They'd Know S0-ABY-163

Only a Brief Time, Yet . . .

They were laughing like two children sharing a private joke when the band swung into a slow number. Suddenly, the mood changed. Robin felt the magnetism flowing between them, and it rang a warning bell. Like a startled fawn, she started to withdraw, but strong arms tightened around her, and she was aware of his hard, muscular body against her own.

Very slowly, he kissed her trembling mouth, and somehow she knew how it would be—the culmination of all her dreams. A tingling swept through her entire body, and it was only with the greatest willpower that Robin finally pulled away. "No, you mustn't," she murmured. "I don't even know you."

He cupped her chin in his hand and looked into her eyes. "But you will, Robin, you will."

TRACY SINCLAIR
has worked extensively as a photojournalist. She's traveled throughout North America, as well as parts of the Caribbean, South America and Europe. *Paradise Island* is her first Silhouette Romance.

Dear Reader:

Silhouette Romances is an exciting new publishing venture. We will be presenting the very finest writers of contemporary romantic fiction as well as outstanding new talent in this field. It is our hope that our stories, our heroes and our heroines will give you, the reader, all you want from romantic fiction.

Also, *you* play an important part in our future plans for Silhouette Romances. We welcome any suggestions or comments on our books and I invite you to write to us at the address below.

So, enjoy this book and all the wonderful romances from Silhouette. They're for *you!*

Karen Solem
Editor-in-Chief
Silhouette Books
P.O. Box 769
New York, N.Y. 10019

TRACY SINCLAIR
Paradise Island

Silhouette Romance
Published by Silhouette Books New York
America's Publisher of Contemporary Romance

SILHOUETTE BOOKS, a Simon & Schuster Division of
GULF & WESTERN CORPORATION
1230 Avenue of the Americas, New York, N.Y. 10020

Copyright © 1980 by Tracy Sinclair
Map copyright © 1980 by Tony Ferrara

Distributed by Pocket Books

ISBN: 0-671-57039-0

First Silhouette printing October, 1980

10 9 8 7 6 5 4 3 2 1

America's Publisher of Contemporary Romance

Printed in the U.S.A.

Paradise
Island

Chapter One

Robin O'Neill stood at the railing of the luxury liner *Island Queen* and looked out over the Pacific. There were at least a million stars glittering like tiny diamonds in the black velvet sky and a full moon shone down on an ocean as calm as its name. The giant ship's prow cut smoothly through inky waters leaving a boiling white trail of foam in its wake. And in the ghostly moonlight, flying fish made silvery arcs before disappearing into the darkness.

They were headed into tropical waters and everyone was in a festive mood. Balmy breezes whispering of romance caressed the passengers as they strolled in and out of brilliantly lighted salons, laughing and murmuring together, the women in delicate, diaphanous gowns that swirled around their ankles and the men handsome in dinner jackets and gleaming white shirts.

Music escaped from the ballroom every time the

doors were thrust open and floated sweetly on the air for a moment before drifting out to sea. And before the heavy steel doors swung shut, couples could be glimpsed floating dreamily around the polished floor.

Robin surveyed the romantic scene and shivered with pure joy. Even now she could scarcely believe her good fortune. She kept pinching herself surreptitiously, sure that she would wake up and find she had just imagined herself on an ocean liner bound for Hawaii. How was it possible that she, Robin O'Neill, who had never been out of San Francisco in all of her almost nineteen years, could be so lucky? Luxury cruises were for the rich—everyone knew that—not for orphans without a penny to their names.

She settled more comfortably against the railing and watched the dancers circling the floor. The rhythm was infectious and her toe started to tap in time with the music. What fun if she could join them. But the next minute she started to giggle. A short pink shift and braided white sandals were definitely not proper attire for a party! It didn't matter, though—just being here was enough. She was content to be a spectator.

Suddenly a voice from the darkness said, "Hello, youngster, does your mother know you're out prowling around?"

Robin was so sure no one would notice her in the shadows that she jumped guiltily. Turning quickly, she discovered a tall man in a red-and-white striped T-shirt and white duck pants. His piercing dark eyes looked quizzically at her out of a lean, tanned face, and a lock of unruly black hair fell over his forehead.

He looks like a pirate, was Robin's first thought. She could almost imagine him climbing over the side of the ship, a knife clenched in his gleaming white teeth.

Which was silly, of course. Common sense told her he was undoubtedly just part of the crew, but he didn't look like an ordinary sailor. In proper clothes he could have been a Spanish grandee or a Roman prince. There was arrogance and breeding in the elegant planes of his face.

Without realizing it, she was staring at him wordlessly and her reaction was matched by his. The laughter went out of his dancing dark eyes as he looked at her, pale and delicate in the moonlight. Suddenly she had the strangest feeling that they were alone on the ship. And that it was meant to be that way. This wasn't a chance meeting—it had been preordained way back in the mists of time. Even though she had never seen him before, Robin knew she had been waiting for this man all her life.

As if the same magic gripped him, he moved toward her almost instinctively and she swayed helplessly, waiting for the inevitable. But then a door slammed in the distance, bringing her abruptly to her senses.

She shivered and leaned against the railing, unaccountably frightened by the powerful attraction of this fascinating stranger. Casting wildly about for something to break the spell, she recalled his greeting. "I'm not a youngster," she told him in a voice that trembled slightly in spite of her efforts to control it.

His eyes flicked briefly over the tender curves outlined by her short pink sun dress and the laughter returned to his eyes. "Obviously. But what are you doing out here all alone, little Cinderella? Didn't anyone invite you to the ball?"

He was teasing her, and in a way Robin was glad. At least he wasn't looking at her with that brilliant, compelling gaze that had mesmerized her for just a moment. But she didn't want to be treated like a child either. He was really a very aggravating man and she vowed to put him in his place.

In her loftiest manner, Robin said, "I don't have time to waste dancing. I'm a governess and I have a small boy to take care of." Then, in case he wondered why she wasn't paying attention to duty, she hastily added, "He's just fallen off to sleep and I came out for a breath of fresh air."

"Ridiculous! I don't believe a word of it! You are Cinderella and your wicked stepmother banished you to the promenade deck. And the evil witch sent your fairy godmother on a wild goose chase to the galley looking for a pumpkin. Pity she didn't check with me first—I could have saved her the trip. There isn't a pumpkin within two thousand miles. Do you think she could make do with a pineapple?"

In spite of herself, Robin laughed. His nonsense was infectious and put her more at ease. "You know what? You're absolutely crazy. Who are you anyway?"

"Don't you recognize me, you silly girl? I'm your Prince Charming!" And he swept her into his arms and twirled her round and round the deck, saying, "I'm sorry the dance floor is so small. I see I'll have to enlarge the palace."

"Not at all, my lord," she answered, getting into the spirit. "I think it's quite cozy."

The music from the ballroom was muted but clear enough to be heard easily. The orchestra was playing a lively tune from a Broadway show and they started to sing the words at the same time, which for no special reason struck them both as funny. He was a marvelous dancer and Robin followed him effortlessly, enjoying the whole silly situation.

They were laughing like two children sharing a private joke when the band swung into a slow number. Automatically he matched his steps to the music and drew her closer. Suddenly the mood changed. Robin felt the same magnetism flowing between them and it rang a warning bell. Like a startled fawn, she started to withdraw, but strong arms tightened around her and she was aware of his hard muscular body against her own.

This time she hadn't the strength to resist and relaxed helplessly in his embrace. When his lips brushed the soft silken hair off her forehead, she lifted her face to his. Very slowly, he kissed her trembling mouth, and somehow she knew how it would be—the culmination of all her dreams.

A tingling swept through her entire body, and it was only with the greatest of willpower that Robin finally pulled away. "No, you mustn't," she murmured, "I don't even know you."

He cupped her chin in his hand and looked deep into her eyes. "But you will, darling, you will."

His gaze was so intent that Robin's eyelashes fluttered like delicate feathers against her flushed cheeks. Did he really mean that? Or, for that matter, did she want him to? She was confused by wildly conflicting emotions and didn't know what to say. While she struggled for words, she sensed a change come over him. Glancing up, she saw him looking over her shoulder, and there was an expression on his face she couldn't decipher.

"I have to go now, but I'll see you tomorrow night. Meet me down on the tourist deck at nine o'clock—that's where the fun is. There's a little lounge with a jukebox. I'll see you there." And he started to leave.

"Wait!" she cried, "I . . . I don't know if I can."

He ran his finger playfully down her tilted nose. "No excuses—just be there! I'll be waiting for you—don't be late."

Robin was too disconcerted by his sudden departure to take offense at his autocratic manner. "But I don't even know your name," she called after him.

As he disappeared into the shadows, his mocking voice floated back to her. "Prince Charming," it said.

Of all the maddening men! She turned around to see what had driven him away so suddenly and saw a worried-looking man hurrying toward her. She had never seen him before and wondered what he wanted, but he wasn't looking for her. He passed right by Robin and sped after the mystery man. Of course, she thought, ordinary seamen weren't supposed to be up on the first-class deck—just the officers. If he were caught he would probably be in a lot of trouble. Oh, dear, she hoped they didn't catch him! Not that it mattered to her—personally, that is. She certainly wasn't going to meet him tomorrow night—a man she didn't even know and a crazy one at that. Still, he really was amusing.

She smiled in the darkness as she remembered their rollicking waltz around the deck. What a pair they made, he in white ducks and she in a sun dress. Not exactly a royally clad couple. Yet . . . he made her feel like she was garbed in satin.

Her eyes grew dreamy and she was in his arms again, feeling his lips against hers, urgent yet tender. Then she came to her senses. Don't make a big thing out of it, Robin told herself firmly. It was just a kiss. Don't be a silly child and try to make a romance out of what was a mere casual encounter—nothing more, nothing less.

But as long as that's all it was, what would be the harm in seeing him again?

By the time she got to her cabin, Robin had succeeded in convincing herself that she really ought to meet him the next night, if only to prove to herself that he wasn't anything special. With other people around and under the bright lights of the lounge, he would prove to be just an ordinary sailor. But as she brushed her long shining hair and gazed dreamily into the mirror, it wasn't her own face she saw. A lean, dark pirate stared back, his mouth curled up sardonically. A delicious shiver ran up Robin's spine and she reached hurriedly to turn out the light and jump into bed.

An hour later she was still wide awake, staring exasperatedly at the ceiling. Why couldn't she get that man out of her mind? He meant absolutely nothing to her, she assured herself, and after the ship docked day after tomorrow, she would never see him again. They lived in two completely different worlds. She would go back to San Francisco and he would go on sailing the seven seas, meeting other women and undoubtedly kissing them in the moonlight. Which was perfectly all right with her, of course. Her own life was full enough without him.

Just a few short weeks ago she had been helping out with the younger children at the orphanage and Hawaii was merely a romantic little dot on the map. Robin crossed her arms in back of her head and reflected on the strangeness of fate.

Her life had never been filled with material things but, perhaps because she hadn't known the kind of home that other children take for granted, she had been perfectly happy where she was. And it could have been a lot worse. The Sisters of Charity orphanage was immaculate and well run by women who were kind and truly cared about their charges.

Robin was five years old when she had come to the orphanage and her case was rather unique. Her father had died shortly after Robin's birth and her mother, who was far from well, had struggled for five years to work and care for her at the same time. Finally, when the burden became impossible, Mrs. O'Neill brought the child to the Sisters of Charity and begged them to look after her.

She had been an enchanting youngster with cornsilk hair and pansy-blue eyes and would probably have been adopted in a matter of weeks, but Mrs. O'Neill made it clear from the start that she would never give her consent. It was desperation that made her give up the child, but she always hoped their separation would be only temporary. Maybe her health would improve so that she could get a better job, or perhaps . . . well, hope springs eternal.

It didn't work out that way, though, and the years passed. Robin settled into the routine of the orphanage and soon it was the only life she remembered. Everyone loved her for her friendliness and sunny disposition and soon she was the favorite of both children and teachers alike. That was really an accomplishment because children don't usually like anyone who is considered "teacher's pet." But Robin had been the exception.

Not that she had been an angel by any means! She got into more than her share of mischief and, since she was usually the ringleader, spent a good part of her time in disgrace. Like the time she led her little band in a midnight raid on the kitchen, where they put salt in the sugar bowl and sugar in the salt shakers, waiting in rapture next morning for Sister Celia to taste her coffee. The good Sister always used three spoons of sugar and the look on her face more than made up for the resultant punishment.

For that little episode Robin had lost her privileges for two weeks. But the time she instigated the pillow fight brought even more dire punishment. How could they have known all those feathers would clog the vacuum cleaner so it would have to go into the shop for repairs?

Robin grinned in the darkness as she recalled those childish escapades. Yes, it had been a good life, and the Sisters saw to it that she also had regular visits with her mother. Sometimes they went to the DeYoung Museum in Golden Gate Park or perhaps down to Fisherman's Wharf to watch the boats come in with their catch of wriggling crabs and sleek, shining petrale. Mrs. O'Neill tried to plan something different for each outing and nothing was too much trouble if she thought it would please the child.

Robin loved her mother and enjoyed these sallies into the outside world but she was never sorry to return to the orphanage. The children were always waiting to hear about her day and it was like coming home to a big family. What she had never realized was that their visits formed the bright spot in her mother's existence.

When she was twelve, Mrs. O'Neill died, and by that time there was no question of adoption. Who would take a child that age? It didn't matter, though—by this time she was as much a fixture as Sister Josephine or Sister Helene. It was the only home she knew and the other children were her brothers and sisters.

It wasn't until she was about sixteen that the Sisters recognized the problem they would eventually have to face. It troubled them and Robin knew about the many worried discussions they held over her. *She* was content with life the way it was but they realized she was growing up and the winds of change were blowing.

One day Sister Helene said, "Sister Josephine, I don't think we can put it off much longer, we simply have to decide on Robin's future. I hate to think of losing her. My goodness, I don't know what this place would be like without her, but we've got to let her go. She has a whole life ahead and it would be selfish to try and keep her caged up here like some exotic little bird."

"Oh, come now, Sister Helene, you make it sound like this is a prison. I don't know of a happier child anywhere than Robin."

"But that's the trouble—she isn't a child any longer. When I looked at her today I suddenly saw an enchanting young woman emerging and it frightened me. Robin is completely unsophisticated. Living here with us all these years has given her no experience with the world and yet she has to go out and make her own living. What's going to happen to her? I'm terribly afraid that she is going to attract men like bees to a honeycomb."

"I know what you mean." The other nodded her head. "The grocery boy delivers if we just call up for a box of salt." An unwilling smile crossed her face. "It's a mixed blessing, though. After he's made his delivery, he hangs around the kitchen getting in everyone's way while he hopes for the tiniest glimpse of Robin."

"If only she had a father or brother to look out for her." Sister Helene sighed. "Or at least she could have been plain-looking. Why did she have to turn out to be such a beauty?"

"She was a beautiful child," Sister Josephine said

drily, "what did you expect? But at least we have a little time yet. After all, she's only sixteen."

"That's cold comfort, the way time seems to be whizzing by."

However, this conversation had ended like all the others because there didn't seem to be any solution. And time did indeed whiz by. One day a couple of years later, Sister Josephine happened to see an advertisement in the newspaper for a governess.

"Why, this is absolutely perfect!" she exclaimed. "Robin is marvelous with children and it says here, 'room and board.' She would live in a proper home with a nice family and they'd supervise her comings and goings. Thank goodness, I do believe our problems are solved."

Robin, however, was less sanguine about the matter, especially after the Sisters got through fussing over her. They had taken one of her oldest and plainest dresses and let the hem completely down so that it was only inches above her slender ankles. And as if that wasn't bad enough, they parted her silky blond hair into two braids and wound them tightly around her head.

Robin indignantly surveyed herself in the mirror, her violet blue eyes darkening with displeasure. "What did you do to me? I look like I came out of somebody's album. If *I* had a job to fill I certainly wouldn't hire *me!*"

"You look very neat," Sister Josephine chided her.

"Neat?" Robin exploded. "I look like a museum piece! Why can't I wear a decent dress, and what's wrong with my hair the normal way?"

The two older women exchanged a glance. The girl was completely without guile or conceit, so how could they explain to her that there were many women who wouldn't welcome the threat her radiant young beauty might seem to offer. This position was heaven-sent and they meant to get her safely placed.

Sister Helene said primly, "You don't want to appear flamboyant, my dear. After all, you have to consider the impression you will make on your prospective employers."

"Well, if they have someone like Mary Poppins in mind, I'm sure to get the job," Robin muttered rebelliously.

"You look perfectly charming. Now come along—we mustn't be late for our appointment."

"We?" Robin was incredulous. "Do you mean to say you're coming with me?"

"Of course. Sister Josephine and I are both going with you. We want to meet Mrs. Dahlgren and see what kind of a home you'll be living in. You don't think we would just turn you loose in the world without checking the circumstances thoroughly, do you?"

"But this is crazy!" Robin raged. "You don't have to lead me by the hand. What will the Dahlgrens think?"

Sister Helene was adamant. "They'll think you are a properly brought up young lady, and if the surroundings are what we consider suitable, I'm sure you will get the position."

And that's exactly what happened. Even Mrs. Dahlgren, a slightly plump but exquisitely groomed lady, was somewhat surprised. She had intended to interview quite a few applicants before making up her mind, but unaccountably she found she had engaged Robin on the spot. Sister Helene and Sister Josephine were favorably impressed by the Dahlgren household, and once they made up their minds, it was all over.

They were a family of four—Mr. and Mrs. Dahlgren,

their twenty-year-old daughter Pauline, and the baby, Richard, who was five. When Robin met him, she knew why he needed a governess. He was adorable but high spirited and too much for his mother to cope with. Although Mrs. Dahlgren didn't mention the fact that he had come as a great surprise to her, it was obvious that he was a late-in-life baby.

When he was brought in briefly to meet his new governess, everyone promptly fell in love with him. His tousled blond curls made it evident that he favored his mother in coloring, although her hair was now aided quite a bit by the beauty salon. But his temperament was all boy. From his wide, engaging grin to his scraped knees, he was a complete love, and Robin was enchanted with him.

She took his proffered little hand and said, "My name is Robin and I hope we're going to be very good friends."

He inspected her gravely, decided he liked what he saw, and said, "My name's Richard, but only my grandma calls me that. Mommy calls me Dicky. Will you call me Dicky too?"

"I think I'll call you Dicky Bird after a song I once heard. Is that all right?"

He gave what could only be called a chortle. "That's silly. I'm not a bird—*you* are. You're a robin and that's a bird." And then, spreading his arms wide, he started to swoop around the room in circles. "Look at me. I can fly, I can fly!"

"Young man, if you break that Ming bowl you are going to be in very deep trouble," his mother warned.

Before he could precipitate a disaster, Robin swept him up in her arms, and they collapsed on the carpet, giggling like two children.

Sister Josephine gave Sister Helene a satisfied look and they both rose. Their mission was accomplished. Robin's future, at least the immediate one, was assured, and it was time to take their leave.

"It was a great pleasure to meet you, Mrs. Dahlgren," Sister Helene said, "and we will arrange to have Robin's things brought over."

"Oh, yes, her things." Mrs. Dahlgren looked doubtfully at Robin in her strange getup. "As I told you, we're going to the Islands shortly and she's going to need . . . well, never mind. She's about Pauline's size and I'm sure we can fit her out comfortably. That girl has clothes in her closet that she's never even worn, and every time you look for her she's out buying more. I'm afraid she is as spoiled as this one," Mrs. Dahlgren sighed, her jeweled fingers waving toward Dicky.

But Pauline wasn't spoiled at all. She was a charming, levelheaded young lady, though with a strong mind of her own, like her little brother, and scant patience with her mother's caprices.

Robin liked her as soon as they met—a feeling that was reciprocated by the other girl—and they were immediate friends in spite of being different as night and day. Pauline was as dark as Robin was fair, a tall slender girl with dark brown, almost black hair cut in the latest style. Her generous mouth and high cheekbones gave her the look of a fashion model—not really beautiful, but very chic.

She had been to the best schools and raised in the lap of luxury, but she was completely down to earth, and that was the basis of most of her arguments with her mother. Mrs. Dahlgren was a bit of a social climber and Pauline flatly refused to go along with her plans. Like the trip to Hawaii, for instance.

"For heaven's sake, Mother, why do we have to go by ship? It only takes five hours by plane."

"I simply don't understand you, Pauline. Most girls your age would jump at the chance for a lovely sea voyage."

"Lovely, my foot!" Pauline answered inelegantly. "Five deadly days of boredom, that's what it is. Nobody takes those cruises except a bunch of old fogies who can barely totter around the deck. And besides, you're not fooling me one bit. The only reason you want to take this particular ship is because you heard that Calvin Carrington the third is going to be aboard."

"Nothing of the kind," her mother answered airily. "I'll admit that it was a happy coincidence, since we rented the home next to his in Diamond Head. But what's wrong with wanting to get acquainted with your neighbors? Since we both just *happen* to be on this cruise, we will probably be the greatest of friends by the time we reach Honolulu."

"How friendly would you be if he wasn't the greatest catch in the western hemisphere?" Before her mother could get an angry word in, Pauline explained to Robin, "It isn't only that he's an unmarried multimillionaire—there must be a few of those around—but he's handsome and young to boot."

"How young?" Robin asked curiously.

"I don't know—somewhere in his thirties, I think," Pauline said.

"Thirty-four," Mrs. Dahlgren murmured before she could stop herself and at least had the grace to look self-conscious.

Pauline started to laugh. "There, you see what I mean? What's the exact date, Mother—maybe we should send him a birthday card."

"Pauline, you will kindly watch your tongue! I don't know why you have developed this great aversion to Mr. Carrington. Any normal girl would leap at the chance of meeting him. The fact that he's rich has nothing to do with it. I just think it would be fascinating to hear all about his cattle ranches and sugar plantations and the rest."

"Don't forget his yacht," Pauline said sarcastically.

"Well, yes, of course, the yacht. I understand it's quite huge."

"Too bad it's in dry dock," Pauline commented. "Otherwise he'd be on it and we'd be on the plane. Mother, won't you reconsider? Calvin Carrington is probably such a conceited bore that even *you* wouldn't like him—with *all* his money."

Mrs. Dahlgren was becoming exasperated. "That's enough, Pauline! We're going on the ship and if you meet Mr. Carrington I shall expect you to be civil at the very least. Although I would hope you'd be more than that."

"Honestly, Mother"—this was a continuing complaint—"I wish you'd stop trying to marry me off. I know I'm not gorgeous but I don't exactly scare small children in the streets and I do have my share of boyfriends. And besides, I'm not precisely an old maid yet!"

But Pauline needn't have worried about Calvin Carrington. To Mrs. Dahlgren's extreme chagrin, neither she nor any of the other passengers ever caught a glimpse of him. It was well known that he occupied one of the two luxury suites on board—a magnificent apartment with soft couches and wide picture windows instead of portholes. That much could be glimpsed when the door was partially open, but no one ever got any further.

As soon as she was settled, Mrs. Dahlgren paid a courtesy call, but was greeted by Mr. Carrington's male secretary, who politely but firmly told her that his employer was indisposed. She never got over the threshold.

From discreet inquiries, she discovered that Mr. Carrington was recovering from the flu, which was the reason for his presence aboard. He usually traveled by private plane, but this time had decided on a sea voyage to get away from the constantly ringing telephone and the press of business that a tycoon always encounters. And although it wasn't explicitly stated, he obviously wanted to avoid people as well, since he even took his meals in his suite.

Mrs. Dahlgren was extremely disconcerted but not to the point of giving up hope. Sooner or later she was sure he would get bored enough to come out of his lair, so she bided her time, although not very patiently.

Pauline, on the other hand, had all but forgotten his existence. Much to her surprise, the cruise was turning out to be great fun. There were many elderly people aboard, but there was also a group her own age. And what she found even more interesting—the young officers of the ship took their meals with the passengers and also spent their evenings with them. They were supposed to divide their time dancing with all the ladies, but Pauline found herself paired almost exclusively with a young first officer named Michael Browning.

He was an excellent dancer and they made a handsome couple as they circled the floor, his blond head

bent over her dark one. Pauline was having the time of
her life and more than once blessed Calvin Carrington
for keeping her mother occupied if only by his absence.
Pauline knew that her mother would undoubtedly have
considered Michael Browning completely unsuitable
for her daughter—even as a dancing partner. But
Pauline enjoyed his company tremendously and her
group of young people stayed up every night partying
till the wee small hours and sleeping late in the
morning.

Robin, quite the reverse, was up with Dicky every
day at the crack of dawn. Like most small boys, he was
an early riser, but she didn't mind. The cruise was like a
dream come true and she didn't want to waste a minute
of this glorious experience.

Usually she was so tired by nightfall that she fell
asleep as soon as her head hit the pillow but this
evening was different. Tonight she was wide awake
because of a pair of teasing dark eyes and a low,
caressing voice. Wasn't that ridiculous?

If I don't go to sleep pretty soon I won't be able to
get up in the morning, Robin told herself, and then
proceeded to toss and turn some more. But eventually
she drifted off and it seemed only a few winks later that
Dicky was shaking her shoulder.

"Get up, Robin, I'm hungry. I want breakfast."

She opened one eye and regarded him reluctantly.
He wasn't really hungry, she knew—he just wanted
company. "What time is it?"

"I don't know but I'm starving almost to death—look
at me!" And he clutched his little stomach with both
hands and fell to the carpet, moaning in mock pain.

Robin laughed and jumped out of bed. "You're a

little faker. If you eat two bites I'll be very much surprised." But she dressed hurriedly and took him down to breakfast.

They were always the first ones in the dining room and sometimes had it practically all to themselves. Most of the first-class passengers slept quite a bit later and then had their coffee or tea brought right to their cabins. It invariably was accompanied by luscious wedges of papaya from the Islands or fragrant slices of ripe pineapple.

There were always a few people, of course, who preferred a proper meal served at a table set with snowy white linen. They usually referred to themselves as "morning people" and that was certainly the category small boys fell into.

After breakfast, Robin asked Dicky what he wanted to do. "This is our last day, remember, so we'd better make the most of it. Tomorrow morning we dock in Honolulu."

"I don't want to get off the boat," he said. "I want to stay on—I'm having fun."

"So am I, Dicky Bird," she answered softly, "but even good things come to an end."

"No, I don't want it to," he said stubbornly.

She finally promised to make this their very best day yet. And it was indeed. They swam in the pool and played games on deck and even sighted the awesome black fin of a shark. Lunch was special too. Dicky got to choose his own meal, complete with two desserts and no vegetables. Then it was back to the stern for a last look at the flying fish.

The day flew by on happy wings and was over almost before she knew it. By the time Dicky was safely tucked in bed, Robin discovered it was nearly nine o'clock—the hour her mystery man had commanded her to appear.

She had changed her mind since last night and had decided not to go, but all afternoon she fought a losing battle with herself. Should she keep the date? It was completely out of the question and of course she wasn't going!

But still . . . he was expecting her and it really wouldn't be polite to let him wait and wait. Maybe she ought to go just to tell him she wasn't coming. No, that was crazy! If she was there, how could she say she wasn't coming? All right, then, she'd go to meet him but she'd tell him she couldn't stay.

With that settled to her satisfaction, Robin turned her attention to the really important matter of what to wear. Gradually the small cabin started to resemble a clothing store as she pulled things out for inspection. The white jeans? She shook her head. The green sun dress? No, much too *jeune fille*. Tonight it would never occur to him to call her "youngster," Robin vowed.

Finally, after much deliberation, she decided on a pale yellow silk that had been one of Pauline's and probably very expensive—a dress that looked like nothing on the hanger but was transformed into a creation on her slender figure. It was a simple frock but it clung to her like a caress, and the color was nothing short of sensational against her pale hair and golden tan.

Robin kept smoothing her skirt nervously as she sped down the wide staircase to the tourist deck. What if he wasn't even there? Her steps faltered as the terrible thought occurred to her for the first time. But it was possible, wasn't it? Maybe it was just a line he gave to all the girls, secure in the knowledge that they wouldn't take him seriously. "Meet me down on the tourist deck at nine o'clock." Big joke! How humiliating if he didn't show up.

Should she turn around and go back? Would it be better to pretend they'd never met and that last night was just something that happened in a dream? But she knew she could never convince herself of that. He was flesh and blood and, unfortunately, so was she. The man who held her in his arms was no figment of her imagination. She could still feel his lips, strong and sure against her own.

There was music coming from a lighted salon up ahead and, after a long moment, Robin made her way toward it. She couldn't turn back now even if she wanted to. No argument she could muster was strong enough to withstand this fierce need to see him one more time, no matter what the cost.

The lounge was packed with young people, all in a holiday mood. Some were sitting around small tables, laughing and talking—others were dancing to the lively music of a garishly lit jukebox in the corner. They all seemed to know each other and she felt like an outsider, standing alone in the doorway. And then she saw him walking toward her and all her doubts were drowned in a wave of pure happiness.

"Hello, Cinderella." He took her elbows and smiled down at her—that same crooked smile she had seen in her mirror. "You're late. Don't let it happen again."

"I . . . well . . . I wasn't sure I was coming," she stammered.

He threw his head back and laughed exultantly, teeth

gleaming white against a deep tan. "Nonsense! You've been counting the hours and you know it."

It was true, of course, but Robin was indignant. "You're mighty sure of yourself, aren't you?"

"Not at all, I just know the story by heart. Wasn't Cinderella eager to meet the prince?"

"And that's another thing. I do wish you'd stop calling me Cinderella."

He put a hard-muscled arm lightly around her waist. "Come on, I have a table for two over in the corner. Let's go sit down and discuss it."

When they were seated, Robin said, "Don't you think it's time we introduced ourselves properly? I don't even know your name."

He grinned at her. "Sure you do. I'm your Prince Charming."

"If you say that one more time I'm going to get up and walk out of here," she warned.

He put his hand over hers and said, "No, don't do that. I'll be good." And then, very seriously, although his eyes were dancing with hidden amusement, he added, "What do you want to know?"

"Well, your name to begin with."

"Why is that important?" he asked. "Shakespeare said, 'What's in a name?' and he was a very perceptive fellow."

"So was Kipling," she flashed back. *He* said, 'Them that asks no questions isn't told a lie,' but that's not the basis for a very firm friendship."

He gave her a startled glance. "Touché." Leaning forward, he took her face in his hands and looked deep into her eyes, compelling her to look back at him. All the laughter was gone and he was dead serious as he told her, "Listen carefully, little darling. I will never tell you a lie because I have a feeling our friendship is going to be very firm indeed."

She never knew how to respond to these sudden shifts in mood and her cheeks flushed as she sat back in her chair and nervously fiddled with the edge of her sash. Why was she always at such a disadvantage with him? He made her feel so young and inexperienced. He couldn't possibly mean all those things he said, so why couldn't she just pass them off with a sophisticated laugh the way Pauline would? The main thing, though, was to keep him from knowing how wildly her heart was thumping.

Striving desperately for a light note, Robin said, "I'm sure you haven't lied, but that's only because you haven't told me anything."

A mask slipped over his face and he was his old sardonic self. "I'm afraid you have no romance in your soul, Cindy, but I'm determined to put some there. Tell me, what's your favorite name? For a man, that is."

She thought for a minute. "David, I think."

"All right, then—I'm David and you're Cindy. How's that?"

Robin laughed helplessly. "I suppose I'll have to settle for that since it's obvious you aren't going to tell me anything about yourself."

"I'll tell you anything you want to know, but right now let's dance. Someone finally found a slow tune on that infernal machine." He rose and held out his arms to her and she went blissfully into them.

He held her close as they circled the floor, his cheek resting gently against her forehead, and they merged into one person. Robin followed his steps as willingly as she would have followed him through life. They were oblivious to the others on the floor and time had no meaning—only each other. When the music finally stopped and he led her back to the table, she didn't know if they had been dancing for an hour or a minute.

"Thank you, Cindy, that was very lovely," he said gently, and for once seemed to mean just that.

They talked and Robin found herself relaxing with him for the first time. He wanted to know everything about her, and she found herself telling him of the orphanage and about her mother. She even told him about her childish escapades, and they laughed over the scrapes she'd gotten into. He seemed so genuinely interested that Robin didn't realize she was doing most of the talking. Somehow the questions she wanted to ask him never came up and he didn't volunteer any information. Was it because she hadn't given him a chance or was there another reason?

Finally she noticed they were almost the last ones in the lounge. It had been a perfect evening and she didn't want it to end, but did he feel the same? All the old doubts rushed forward. Why didn't he ask to see her again? He had seemed so interested, but was that just an act? He still hadn't given her any clue as to how he really felt about her. Maybe he was really bored with her and was just being polite. Better to leave now before she inadvertently let him know how desperately it mattered to her.

She bent her head and concentrated on making imaginary circles on the table with her forefinger. "It must be getting late. I guess I should be getting back," she said.

"I'll take you to your cabin," he answered. Just that. No begging her to stay longer or mention of tomorrow.

He pushed his chair back and Robin got up listlessly. As he rose to join her, there was a faint ripping sound.

He looked over his shoulder and said, "Oh, blast it. Tore my pocket on a nail. But at least I'm glad it was my chair and not yours. It would have been a pity to ruin that beautiful dress."

She inspected the small tear. "It's not so bad, just a ripped seam. If you have time in the morning, bring it to me and I'll fix it in a jiffy. We probably won't be leaving till noon. Dicky's mother isn't up much before that."

It was a small favor she offered but for some reason he seemed touched. He took both of her hands in his and said, "You would do that for me—a sailor you've just met?"

Gratitude wasn't the emotion she'd been seeking and she wasn't willing to settle for it. The last thing she wanted was for him to feel obligated to her. She pulled her hands away and started for the door. "I'd do as much for any friend," she assured him lightly.

It was now obvious that he considered this just a brief shipboard romance, so she would pretend that's all it was to her too. "And what difference does it make that you're a sailor?" she added as he held the door for her. "It's a perfectly honorable profession."

"I've always thought so," he was quick to agree.

Robin hoped she was the picture of nonchalance as she commented brightly, "It must be wonderful to visit all those foreign ports."

They were walking along the moonlit deck and he took her hand and gently swung it back and forth. "Would you like to travel?" he asked.

"Oh, yes. I think everybody would. You don't know how lucky you are."

"I don't know," he said. "It has its disadvantages. For instance, there isn't always a beautiful young lady on board to do your mending. You're really quite wonderful, you know."

"Because I can thread a needle?" She smiled. "You'd be surprised how many of us there are."

They had reached her cabin and Robin turned to say goodbye. He leaned over, caging her between outstretched arms braced against the wall. Her face was clear in the moonlight, but his was in shadows and she couldn't read his expression.

"You're wrong, my dear. There aren't very many people in this world who do something without expecting a reward," he said.

"I think that's terribly cynical," she protested. "Why would you think I'd want anything for doing you a simple favor?"

"Not you, my darling. Never you." His hands dropped to her shoulders and then slid slowly upward, tangling in her hair, moon-washed to a pale gilt. He cradled her face gently in his palms and whispered, "I knew you were very special the minute I saw you."

And then he kissed her—a long, slow kiss that burned itself into her very soul. Glorious rockets and fiery pinwheels went off in her head. This wasn't the end—it was the beginning! How could she have doubted it? He didn't have to put it in words—his kiss told her all she needed to know. Robin twined her arms happily around his neck and gave herself completely to his embrace.

But then he released her, saying, "Goodnight, Cinderella," and he was gone, leaving her alone in the moonlight.

It was like being cast out of paradise and for a moment Robin couldn't understand what had happened. Why had he left her so casually? Was it her fault? Was she wrong to respond to him the minute he demanded it? Perhaps she had scared him off by being too eager.

Or maybe she had been right the first time and he really didn't care at all. It was just a game he played with all the girls, but if they got serious he was off like a shot. That exquisite kiss had thrilled her down to the tips of her fingers but it obviously didn't mean a thing to him.

Tears formed in Robin's eyes and she dashed them away angrily. Well, she'd show him in the morning! She would fix his doggone pocket and let him know that he didn't mean anything to her either. Two could play that game, and let's see how he liked it.

Wearily, she turned and entered the cabin.

Chapter Two

Robin's dreams were troubled and she tossed and turned all night. By the time morning came, bringing Dicky to wake her, she felt tired and dispirited.

"Get up, Robin, we're here. We have to get off the boat." He had completely forgotten his reluctance of the day before and was now eager for a new experience.

"Oh, Dicky Bird, we have hours yet," she groaned.

"No we don't. I want to go now—right this minute."

"How about some breakfast first?' she asked, splashing cold water in the tiny sink. Her eyes were ringed with circles but Robin determined not to think about the reason for them.

"I'd rather go swimming in the ocean. It's different from the one in San Francisco."

She smiled wanly. "It's the same ocean, honey."

"No it isn't. This one has real warm water and lots of

pretty fishes in it and you can find funny shells on the beach. Tommy Burton in my kindergarten class at home brought back a great big shell and when you put it up to your ear you can hear the ocean. Do you think we could find one like that, Robin?"

She looked down at him fondly and told him she was sure they could. All through breakfast his sweetly piping little voice instructed her in the glories of Hawaii as decreed by Tommy Burton. Robin was trying to bestow her full attention and still get a few bites of food into him when his mother appeared unexpectedly at their table.

"Why, Mrs. Dahlgren, I didn't expect you so early," Robin said in astonishment. It was something that had never happened before, which accounted for her surprise.

Robin didn't know it but her employer had been up half the night arguing with her daughter and then was too upset to sleep till her customary hour in the morning. Belatedly, Mrs. Dahlgren had discovered that Pauline was spending almost all her time with Michael Browning and there had been a terrible row. While Pauline couldn't see any harm in it, her mother was of a different opinion. Why, the girl even wanted to invite him to visit while the ship was in port! Mrs. Dahlgren had a frightful headache and was in a temper to match.

"I want to get off this dreadful ship as soon as possible," she snapped. "The whole trip has been a disaster!"

"I'm sorry. Is there anything I can do?" Robin asked wonderingly.

"Yes, you can get Dicky's things together immediately. We're going to leave in half an hour."

"But I thought . . . I mean, you said . . ." She tried again. "Aren't most of the passengers leaving about noon?"

"I don't care what they're doing," Mrs. Dahlgren said peevishly. "They can sail on to Australia, for all I care. Now if you've finished your breakfast, please go up and start packing. One half hour, remember," she warned.

Dicky slipped out of his chair and started jumping up and down. "Hurry up, let's go get ready. Mommy said so."

But Robin just sat there, a stricken look on her face. She had thought to have the whole morning aboard ship. She had told David they weren't leaving till noon. If he did try to find her to say . . . well, even just to say goodbye, she would be gone.

She had spent the whole night thinking about him and still didn't know where she stood. One minute she assured herself his kiss had to mean something but the next minute she was filled with bitter doubts again. How could she bear it, never knowing for sure? This was the end of all her hopes. She didn't even know his name—his *real* name, that is—and he didn't know hers. Once she left the ship, he couldn't find her if he wanted to. But did he want to? She would never know now.

Dicky was pulling at her hand, urging her to hurry, and Robin allowed herself to be tugged to her feet. What else could she do? Mrs. Dahlgren had been very explicit in her orders, and even if Robin snatched a few minutes for herself, what good would it do? She couldn't go down in the hold looking for him. Who would she ask for? It came back to that again. The foolish joke had backfired.

With a heavy heart, Robin finished packing and got

herself and Dicky to the gangplank. Sailors were everywhere—loading cargo, shouting orders down to the dock, dodging nimbly in and out. For a minute there was a wild hope that maybe she'd spot him in the crowd, but it wasn't possible. Mrs. Dahlgren was waiting impatiently for them, and as soon as they arrived she shepherded them down the gangplank.

Mr. Dahlgren was waiting there with the cars. He had flown over the day before, saying that he couldn't spare the time a cruise would take, but Robin knew he just didn't want to.

He was a bluff, hearty man who loved his family and indulged his wife's every whim, but his real interest was business. The *Wall Street Journal* was his favorite reading matter and he was happiest while discussing mergers and stock options with other men. When his wife had proposed taking a house in Honolulu for a whole month, his first reaction had been reluctance at being away from the office that long. But she managed to talk him into it as she did most things.

He was waiting for them now with a broad smile on his face. "Over here, Margaret," he called to Mrs. Dahlgren. "Well, how did everybody enjoy the trip?" He kissed his wife on the cheek, hugged Pauline, and swung Dicky up over his head. With the little boy settled in his arms, he smiled at Robin.

Mrs. Dahlgren said grimly, "I'll tell you about it later. Pauline, you go with Robin and Dicky and take some of the luggage. Your father and I will follow in the other car."

"Oh, oh," Pauline said under her breath. "Poor Dad—is he going to get an earful!"

Robin, who knew nothing about the argument, said, "I don't understand, what's wrong?"

"Mother's on the warpath. First, she wasted the whole cruise trying to track down Calvin Carrington and couldn't even get a glimpse of him, and then she discovered I made friends with a first officer named Michael Browning."

"What's wrong with that?" Robin asked.

"Nothing at all for normal girls, but Mother has her heart set on a millionaire for me—isn't that ridiculous? I swear, she would have loved living back in the Dark Ages, when marriages were arranged. Oh, Robin, I wish you had gotten to know Michael—he's a darling. We had so much fun together and he's so handsome!"

Robin's heart was a cold lump in her breast. She had met a handsome man too—much good it did her, she thought bitterly. Unlike Pauline and her Michael, they'd had so little time together, and now she'd never see him again.

Pauline was bubbling on and on about Michael but Robin turned for a last glimpse out the back window. The car started to move and her eyes misted over. It took all her willpower not to cry, but no one must know. She just couldn't talk about it right now.

Eventually, Pauline would have come out of her rosy haze and noticed something was wrong. If the two girls had been alone, that is. But Dicky was with them and he was the kind of small boy who commands everyone's attention.

"Robin, look at the soldiers—there must be about a million of them," he shouted, almost falling out the window in his excitement.

She hastily pulled him back as his sister said, "Well, not exactly a million, honey—probably just a platoon. There is an army camp here in Honolulu—it's called

Schofield Barracks. Maybe some day Robin and I will take you there. I think they have regular tours."

"That sounds interesting," Robin managed politely.

"A small boy's paradise," Pauline grinned. "Dicky was here a couple of years ago but of course he wouldn't remember it. Now look over there—see all those stores? That's the Ala Moana shopping center, one of the largest shopping malls in the whole world. It has so many stores, you can buy anything from a bikini to a bicycle. You and I will have to go there one day, Robin."

The car sped through unfamiliar streets and Robin's head bobbed from side to side like that of someone at a tennis match. There was so much to see and everything looked tropical and exotic. Soon they started up a wide boulevard lined with big hotels that were the ultimate in luxury.

"That's the Royal Hawaiian," Pauline told her. "It's one of the oldest hotels in Honolulu and was once the grandest. Men used to be turned away if they didn't wear dinner jackets, and of course all the ladies wore long gowns. Very elegant in its day, but the standards are relaxed somewhat now."

"Too bad," Robin commented.

"I suppose. It's still beautiful, though. The dance floor is built right out over the beach. A low stone wall keeps the sand out and you can dance under the stars and watch the rollers break on the shore. Very romantic. And the hotel next door has a giant banyan tree in the courtyard. It's hundreds of years old and so big you can't put your arms even halfway around the trunk."

Stately royal palms rose majestically to the burning

blue sky and in between the measured rows were coconut palms that leaned whichever way the wind blew. Bougainvillea vines carpeted the sides of buildings with brilliant purple and scarlet blooms and hibiscus bushes were covered with flowers of every color imaginable. The tall trees Dicky pointed to were most unusual. A slim trunk was crowned at the very top by a rounded cluster of leaves, like a giant flower on a long straight stem, and the large pear-shaped fruit were grouped under the bottom leaves.

"That's a papaya tree," his sister told him. "Remember that sweet orange fruit you had on the ship? Well, those are the trees it grows on."

Pauline had been to the Islands many times and she was a good tour guide. She explained all the points of interest along the way and Robin was sorry when the ride ended. It was as good as being on a sight-seeing bus. But finally the car turned into a driveway set between two solid walls of greenery. From the street only the top of the roof could be glimpsed, but as they proceeded down the long drive a veritable mansion emerged.

Pauline surveyed the sprawling house with its fountains and statuary and manicured lawns. "Mother has really done herself proud this time," she commented wryly. "Poor Dad. I shudder to think how much this month is costing him—just for the pleasure of living next door to Calvin Carrington III. Oh, well, maybe she'll even get to meet him one day. Come on, Robin, let's get rid of all this stuff and go surfing. If I can find the boards, that is."

"I'm afraid I don't know how," Robin told her, "but I can swim."

"No problem, I'll teach you. You'll pick it up in no time."

It didn't take long to do their unpacking, and since Mrs. Dahlgren took a look at Dicky and announced, much to his dismay, that he needed an immediate haircut, Robin was free to go out on the beach with Pauline.

The house really fronted on the ocean, although its main entrance was from the formal terrace that faced the circular drive. A wide hallway led back to a huge living room whose floor-to-ceiling picture windows looked out on the sparkling Pacific lapping with gentle waves on a brilliant white beach.

A wide flagstone patio was furnished with yellow-and-white-striped lawn furniture, and there were fringed yellow canvas umbrellas for those who preferred shade to the dazzling Hawaiian sunshine. In the middle of the patio, on the beach side, three low steps led down to the sand. Robin thought she had never seen anything so beautiful in her entire life.

They had both zipped through their unpacking in record time, unwilling to waste a moment indoors on this glorious day. Now, filled with righteousness because their work was done, they were ready to play. The water was warm yet refreshing and the sun a glowing golden eye. Pauline had managed to locate the surfboards and was giving Robin instructions.

"The idea is to paddle out to where the waves start," she said. "You sit back on your heels with your knees bent like this and paddle with your arms. Then, when you get out far enough, you stand up facing the beach. That's a little tricky but you'll catch on to it. Balance your weight with your legs by putting one foot a little ahead of the other. Then, when a wave comes, you ride it in to shore. Come on, let's try it."

Robin's first attempts were disastrous. She kept sliding off the slippery board, or, when she did finally manage to stand upright, the surfboard would turn broadside into a wave, which would break over her head, smothering her with foam.

"I'm afraid I'm hopeless." She laughed, surfacing and pushing the wet hair out of her eyes.

"No you're not—you're doing fine. You have spirit and that's what counts. Try again—you'll catch on."

And finally Robin did. One minute she was tumbling around in the water and the next minute everything seemed to fall into place. She learned to steer with her legs by shifting her body and soon she was riding the crest like an old pro.

"Pauline, this is marvelous! I feel like I'm soaring . . . like . . . Oh, I don't know. It's wonderful!" Her words lilted back over her shoulder.

Pauline laughed. "I knew you could do it, Champ— you've really got nerve."

Robin was so exhilarated that she kept riding wave after wave, as though she would never get enough. Her arms and legs started to ache from the unaccustomed strain but she wasn't even aware of it. All her problems were washed away by sheer physical exertion. Finally, Pauline had to practically drag her out of the water.

The two girls were lying on the sand resting when Mrs. Dahlgren brought Dicky back. He was indignant at having been dragged away for anything so dumb as a haircut and Robin promised to make it up to him by helping him build a really superior sand castle. Immediately mollified, he ran up to the house to change into his swimsuit.

Mrs. Dahlgren thought she'd change into something cooler also. "But first," she remarked casually, "I think I'll call Mr. Carrington and find out if he would like to have just a quiet little dinner with us this evening."

"Oh, Mother, you're impossible! Can't you give that poor man any peace?" Pauline cried.

"You're being very uncharitable, Pauline. Since he just arrived today, perhaps his staff isn't organized yet. It would be a simple act of neighborliness to invite him over," her mother said.

They argued the matter hotly but Mrs. Dahlgren was not to be dissuaded, and in the end she went up to the house to telephone.

"I don't know why I even bother." Pauline sighed. "Why don't I just give up and make plans for the wedding?"

Robin giggled. "Who knows—maybe you'll even like him," she said flippantly, not knowing how prophetic her words would be.

But Mrs. Dahlgren was destined to be thwarted again. A butler at the Carrington residence informed her that Mr. Carrington was out and he didn't know when to expect him. She was very disgruntled and Robin made sure to give her employer a wide berth that evening.

The next morning Robin woke early to a completely different world. The brilliant sunshine of the day before was gone and in its place were dark storm clouds. Wind was lashing the palm fronds back and forth and the ocean was a mass of little foaming white caps. A large ship steamed slowly out to sea and she watched it somberly, her spirits as low as the barometer. Was he on it, her mystery man?

The weather was depressing and all the misery of

their parting washed over her again. Was he looking back at the island, thinking about her even now, or had he forgotten her the minute he walked away? Was that long sweet kiss meant to say goodbye?

For just a short time yesterday while she was surfing, the ache had subsided. Now it was back in full force. Would she ever stop thinking about him? Would their paths ever cross again? Not likely.

She turned away from the window and squared her drooping shoulders. This moping around had to stop. Life went on and she had to go with it even though it was easier said than done.

The whole household was still asleep—even Dicky, for once, worn out, no doubt, by all the excitement of the preceding day. Robin envied them. She didn't want to wake anyone but further sleep was out of the question, so she decided to go for an early morning swim. It looked like a storm was coming but the air was warm, and if you go swimming you get wet anyway, she reasoned.

Slipping quickly into a white bikini, Robin tiptoed through the house and noiselessly opened the sliding glass door to the patio. The first thing that caught her eye was the two surfboards resting against the low retaining wall, and it gave her an idea. Why not take one out now? Maybe she could recapture some of yesterday's excitement when she had finally managed to stay aloft.

There was a strong current running and by the time Robin had floated the heavy board and managed to climb on, she looked up and discovered that the tide had carried her sideways. She was bobbing around in front of the Carrington house and looked at it curiously. Too bad Mrs. Dahlgren didn't surf, she reflected.

This might be the only way she would ever catch a glimpse of her quarry.

The house was as big as their rented one but completely different in style and much less formal. It was a long, low structure, very Hawaiian in feeling, with lots of wood and glass. Unquestionably a beautiful home, but its most eye-catching feature was the large free-form swimming pool set like a jewel in the middle of the broad terrace. Even under the overcast sky, it sparkled like a giant sapphire.

Lovely wrought-iron chaises and chairs were set around the pool, although their cushions had been removed because of the impending storm, and you could imagine happy people enjoying themselves. It had that kind of atmosphere.

Robin took a last look and then turned to paddle out before the current carried her on down the coast. It was unexpectedly difficult going but she persevered, although her arms were starting to ache. Finally she decided it was far enough out to catch a wave and she tried to stand upright on the slippery board.

It was completely different from the calm sea of yesterday and the polished slice of wood teetered under her. It was almost impossible to keep her balance and several times she nearly pitched headfirst into the rough water. I wonder if this is what it's like to ride a bucking bronco, Robin thought.

Just when it seemed a dunking was inevitable, she managed to keep her balance and the surfboard miraculously stabilized. A ground swell raised her on high and then she was shooting toward shore, exulting over the wild sea that surged beneath her feet.

As she soared over the water, she saw a man racing down the beach toward the ocean. He was waving his

arms and shouting but she couldn't hear anything over
the roar of the elements. He seemed very excited and
began pointing at something beyond her. Confused,
Robin looked over her shoulder and was horrified to
see what the man was trying to tell her.

A giant wave towered high in the air, threatening her
with imminent peril. Like an ugly menacing mouth, it
curled its lip above her head and she could hear the
foam hissing like a thousand snakes. The green water
was unbelievably sinister, as cold and hard as glass.
Petrified with fear, Robin stared helplessly at certain
disaster. And then it broke.

There was a crashing of thunder in her ears and she
was sucked under by powerful crosscurrents, then
shaken and tossed up like a rag doll. She felt the
surfboard slip away and, for just a moment before the
water blinded her, saw it standing straight up in the air.
It poised gracefully for an instant, then fell flat, striking
a glancing blow to the side of her head and right
shoulder. After that there was just darkness.

She awoke to find herself lying on the sand, a
throbbing pain in her temples. A man was kneeling
over her, his face dark with concern. She looked up at
him with difficulty, her eyes still burning from the salt
water. And then, as her vision cleared, she gave a little
cry. It couldn't be, but it was! It was David! He hadn't
sailed over the horizon—he was right here next to her!
Was she dreaming? Or maybe she had drowned and
gone to heaven! A million questions on her lips, Robin
tried to sit up, but he pushed her back none too gently.

"You little fool, what were you doing out on a
surfboard in this sea? Don't you know you could have
killed yourself? Lie still while I see if there are any

broken bones," he commanded as she tried again to sit up.

Far from being glad to see her he seemed downright furious. He was scowling ferociously but his fingers were gentle as they probed her bruised shoulder and cheek. Although she winced a little, he seemed satisfied.

"No broken bones, but you'll be lucky if you don't have one beaut of a black eye. And it would serve you right, pulling a fool stunt like that." He was actually shaking.

She sat up gingerly but found that all of her parts seemed to be in working order. "Thank you for saving my life," she said meekly.

Some of his rage seemed to evaporate and he managed a little smile. "You're entirely welcome. But what the devil were you doing out on a day like this and how did you get here of all places?"

"I woke up early and thought I'd go for a swim. I'm staying next door there." She pointed to the house.

"Next door—you mean at the Dahlgrens'?" He seemed incredulous.

"Yes, do you know them? I take care of their little boy, Dicky. I told you I was a governess." Suddenly something occurred to her. "But what are *you* doing here? I didn't think I'd ever see you again."

His gaze was level and expressionless. "We were supposed to meet yesterday morning, remember? I brought my mending but you were gone. Did you plan it that way?"

"Oh, no!" The words tumbled out of her. "I wanted to see you again, truly I did, but Mrs. Dahlgren decided to leave early in the morning and I didn't know how to find you." She knew she was wearing her heart on her sleeve but she couldn't seem to help it. She loved him and the joy of seeing him again was almost more than she could bear.

At her explanation, his face softened, and he stroked her hair gently. There was tenderness in his eyes and it made Robin feel warm and protected. Then he took her in his arms.

"Little Cindy," he murmured, "you don't know what I went through when I found you were gone."

His words brought pure bliss and Robin sighed happily. All the misery and uncertainty evaporated. He loved her too, and nothing would ever separate them. It had to be fate that brought them together against all odds. And then he kissed her and his lips were warm and satisfying on hers. This was where she belonged, they told her wordlessly, and she agreed. His embrace was so heavenly she could have stayed there forever.

He was the one who drew back first and she remained quietly in his arms as he traced a forefinger over her eyebrows and then gently down the soft curve of her cheek to the sweet full mouth.

"I think it's about time we had a talk, darling. There's something I have to ask you and a lot of things I want to explain. When I think how I almost lost you . . ." His voice was somber. "I see now I should have told you on the ship but there were reasons."

Robin felt happiness surge up inside of her until she was almost suffocated. "It doesn't matter—we found each other again." A thought struck her and she asked anxiously, "Will we have any time together? How soon do you have to be back on the ship?" It would be unthinkable to have him snatched away again now that they were reunited.

"Don't worry about it," he said, brushing a grain of sand off her forehead. He bent toward her once more, but just at that wonderful moment they were interrupted.

A man in sport coat and slacks came hurrying down the beach. He looked familiar somehow, but Robin couldn't quite place him. Then it dawned on her. Of course! It was the man who had disturbed their meeting that first night on the ship. He certainly had a knack for intruding at the wrong times. But how very strange—what was he doing here on the beach?

Before she could ask the question, he approached them. "Someone said there had been an accident, Mr. Carrington. Is everything all right?"

A welter of emotions struggled in David's face—annoyance, impatience . . . and was that embarrassment? "Yes, everything's fine. You can go back to the house, Wilkins."

"Well, if you say so, sir." Wilkins eyed them doubtfully. "There is also a long-distance call from Hong Kong, Mr. Carrington."

Robin looked at him in bewilderment while Wilkins retreated and the awful truth hammered at her new-found happiness. It wasn't possible, was it? It must be a mistake, her heart insisted, but her mind refused the feeble excuse. Her lover, this ordinary sailor, as he called himself, was in reality Calvin Carrington III. The whole thing had been a joke and it was on her. How could anyone be so gullible? It was terribly funny, wasn't it? A multimillionaire and she had offered to mend his coat.

Oh, how he must have been laughing at her! When she remembered how she had poured out her life story, she could have died of embarrassment. No wonder he called her Cinderella and asked her to meet him on the tourist deck where no one would see them. What a lark! A few kisses would keep her happy and create a little diversion until it was time to go back to the rich, glamorous women he usually associated with. Her cheeks were scarlet and she sprang to her feet, aware suddenly of the dull pounding in her temples.

He jumped up at the same time and reached for her. "I didn't want you to find out this way, Cindy. I was going to—"

But she shrank away from him and cut in: "Don't you dare touch me! Your little charade is over, Mr. Carrington, but it must have been very funny while it lasted, wasn't it?"

His brows drew together in a scowl. "Don't be a little idiot—you know it wasn't like that."

"I don't know anything about you except your name. Finally! But now at least I understand why you refused to tell me before. It would have ruined your little game, wouldn't it?"

"Stop acting like a spoiled child and listen to me for a minute. I'll admit it all started as a joke. A beautiful girl alone in the moonlight, a few harmless half-truths"—Robin started to interrupt but he wouldn't let her—"and then I got to know you and I realized you were special. That night in the lounge I didn't want to tell you who I was because I didn't want to spoil something beautiful. We were just a man and a woman falling in love. I wanted you to care about *me*, an anonymous nobody."

"I don't believe you," she cried.

He shook his head in annoyance. "It's the truth and if you weren't being so stubborn you would realize it."

"What would you know about the truth?" she asked

scornfully. I don't believe one word of your lies! If you really felt that way about me, you would have asked where I was staying in Honolulu. You would have wanted to see me again."

"I *expected* to see you again," he shouted impatiently. "You told me you weren't leaving until noon. I was going to tell you everything in the morning, but you were gone."

"If that's true, then how about today?" she asked accusingly. They faced each other angrily and the tension between them was almost tangible. "You had your opportunity just now. You even held me in your arms, but the great Calvin Carrington was still incognito. I may be naive but I'm not a complete fool."

His eyes blazed and he grabbed her by the shoulders, shaking her hard. "You're worse than a fool—you're an obstinate pigheaded little brat! What will it take to convince you, an abject apology? Well, don't count on it, my dear—I'm not one of your teenage boyfriends."

Angry tears welled up in Robin's eyes and she turned and started to run down the wet sand to the Dahlgren house. He hadn't left her any pride, but at least she wouldn't give him the satisfaction of seeing her cry.

"Cindy, wait!" he commanded.

She stopped her headlong flight for just a moment, angry eyes bright with unshed tears. "Don't ever call me that again. My name is Robin!" she shouted back, then turned and ran.

He made no move to follow her, but merely watched her go, a brooding look on his handsome, ruthless face.

Robin's one thought was to get back to the house and hide her head under a pillow. Would she ever get over the shame of this moment? She had practically declared her love in so many words and he had been laughing behind her back—stringing her along because it just happened to amuse him. How could she have been such a fool? Never, never again would she trust another man, Robin vowed.

She felt like a wounded animal whose only desire is to creep away alone, but it wasn't to be. Dicky met her at the door and he was bubbling over with plans for the day.

"Where have you been, Robin? I looked all over the house and you weren't anywhere. Mommy says it's going to rain today and I can't go swimming, so we can go to the movies. It's all about cowboys and afterward we can have sodas, only I'm not supposed to spill anything on my new shirt."

He was jumping up and down with anticipation and she managed to smile at him. It took a tremendous effort, because she thought she would surely die of the pain in her heart, but he was too excited to notice anything different about her. All he could think of was this new adventure.

At first Robin didn't see how she could possibly face anyone—even Dicky. But then she realized she had a job to do even though her life was shattered beyond repair. She had practically thrown herself at a man, but fortunately no one in the house knew and pride demanded she keep it from them. Whatever pride she had left, that is.

Besides, it wasn't the little boy's fault. He was looking at her so expectantly, waiting for her to share his pleasure. She didn't want to spoil his happiness so she swallowed the tears that threatened and said, "That sounds like a wonderful day, honey."

And at least it would be good to get out of the

house—to get as far away from *him* as she could. What she really wanted was to go back to San Francisco, but since that wasn't possible, an afternoon at the movies would have to do. One good thing about it was that she wouldn't have to pretend in the darkened theater.

Dicky was really a godsend that day, demanding all her attention as he did and not giving her time to dwell on her troubles. He dogged her footsteps, barely giving her time to bathe or dress, much less think, and he chattered incessantly. Finally it was time to leave, and not a minute too soon for the small boy. He was in a positive fever of impatience.

The movie was everything he said it would be and Robin smiled at his rapt little face, totally engrossed by the giant screen. Afterward they discussed it over chocolate sodas and Dicky gave his final stamp of approval. "Boy, the deputy sure showed those bad guys. *Pow! Pow! Pow!*" And he polished off three imaginary foes with a make-believe six-shooter.

The day had been a complete success as far as Dicky was concerned and he was too young to notice that Robin's face was sad in repose. She tried to appear normal, although she was suspended somewhere between numbness and pain, but sooner or later the ice around her heart would melt, and that's what she dreaded most. Would she still be able to keep up appearances then?

Fortunately, Dicky did most of the talking. He was wound up like a clock, and when they reached home he ran ahead of her into the house, eager to tell about his adventure.

"Mommy, Pauline, where are you? Want to hear about the movie?"

Mrs. Dahlgren appeared, her manner rather distracted. "Oh, Dicky, you're back already," she said vaguely.

Pauline came in and fondly ruffled the small boy's hair. "You will have to forgive Mother," she told Robin. "She's in a state of shock. You won't believe it, but the elusive Mr. Carrington finally returned her call, and when she invited him to dinner, he accepted."

Robin turned white. She tried to speak but her voice came out almost in a whisper. "When . . . when is he coming?"

"Tonight—wouldn't that kill you?"

Yes, Robin thought, turning away so they wouldn't see her face, it probably would. She wondered if he planned to tell about their meeting on the ship. It would make marvelous dinner conversation—especially those tender moments in the tourist lounge. They could all have a good laugh over it. Imagine Robin taking him for an ordinary sailor! Well, the joke was on her, all right, but at least she didn't have to stay and be humiliated in person.

"Dicky's pretty tired, Mrs. Dahlgren. I'll take him up and pop him in the bathtub. He can have an early dinner in the nursery since you're having company. And I'll have mine with him, if it's all right with you," she added. "I'm rather tired too."

"Don't you want to meet the famous Mr. Carrington?" Pauline asked.

Robin averted her face. "No thank you," she murmured.

Dicky made a token protest, but he was truly all tuckered out. After a good scrubbing in a warm tub, he could barely stay awake through dinner. His eyelids kept drooping against his rosy cheeks.

"Finish your string beans and then you can have dessert," Robin urged him.

"Why? You didn't eat yours," he protested.

It was true. She had barely been able to get a mouthful past the lump in her throat.

Sounds of laughter drifted in from the distant living room and Robin pretended she didn't hear them, willing herself not to try and distinguish that one special voice. If she was lucky, she told herself, she would never hear it again.

Suddenly, there was an actual pain in her breast and she got up and walked to the open window. The cool breeze soothed her flushed face as she studied the view, but the ocean was black in the moonlight—as black as her despair.

"I can't eat anymore," Dicky complained.

"All right, honey, you don't have to. You did pretty well," she told him. "I'll just take these trays down to the kitchen."

On her way through the hall, Robin couldn't help hearing the voices in the living room, but she tried to close her ears to the sound. Just a few more minutes and she would be able to slip back to her room. She had almost accomplished her purpose when luck turned against her.

As she was gliding noiselessly through the hall, Pauline spied her and called out, "Robin, come meet our guest."

Robin turned to ice. How could she face him in front of the Dahlgrens? Had he already told them the story? She wanted to sink quietly through the floor, but there was no escape. They were waiting for her expectantly. Her feet felt like lead as she entered the living room, conscious of her simple linen frock and bare legs.

Mrs. Dahlgren and Pauline were both in long silk gowns.

The men stood up and Pauline made the introductions. "Calvin Carrington, I want you to meet Robin O'Neill."

Robin held her breath, scarcely daring to look at him. She felt like a sacrificial lamb waiting for the executioner. What words would he use to destroy her? There was a pause that lasted only a few seconds but seemed like an eternity. Finally, she couldn't stand it anymore and raised her eyes to discover that he had been waiting for her to look up.

There was the familiar heart-tugging smile at the corner of his mouth as he looked directly at her and said, "I'm very happy to meet you."

He hadn't given her away after all! At least she had one small thing to be grateful for. The crisis was averted, but Robin's ears buzzed and she felt suddenly dizzy.

Pauline's voice seemed to come from a great distance as she said, "Come sit down and have a glass of wine with us."

Mrs. Dahlgren frowned. She had noticed Calvin's quickened interest and she now turned her own appraising glance on Robin, whose pallor accentuated the deep violet of her eyes. "Robin has had a long day and she told us before that she was tired. I think she should run along to bed."

It was all the excuse Robin needed, and she had never been more grateful to anyone. She managed to say a quick good night and then almost ran from the room. Her last memory was of Calvin Carrington, one eyebrow raised and a decidedly amused look on his face.

Chapter Three

The next morning Robin and Dicky were having breakfast alone as usual, but to Robin's surprise Pauline joined them before they had even finished their juice.

"I didn't expect to see you so early," Robin told her.

"I forgot to draw my drapes last night and the sun came in and woke me. But that's okay—it's much too nice a day to waste in bed."

"That's what I've been telling you all along."

"You were right and I'm a reformed character. There's another reason, though—I couldn't wait to talk to you."

Pauline was especially bubbly this morning and Robin looked at her curiously. "What's up?" she asked.

"It's about Calvin Carrington. Remember how we joked about him on the ship and said what a real drag he probably was? Well, we were so wrong! It just shows you shouldn't jump to conclusions."

Robin looked down at her plate. "Oh, really," she commented vaguely.

"Yes, he's a perfect love! For one thing, he's gorgeous—didn't you think so? He's so tall and dark with that kind of leashed power behind every movement. I'm telling you, he's so understanding—" She stopped and gave a little laugh. "I mean, you simply have to get to know him. I wish you had joined us last night—he asked about you."

Startled, Robin raised her eyes. "He did? What did he say?"

The phone rang just then and Pauline ran to answer it, so Robin never got a reply to her question. At first they could hear her clear tones from the hall, but then she lowered her voice until the conversation was inaudible. Robin didn't think much about it because Dicky was keeping up his usual steady chatter, but when the other girl returned to the table, she seemed to avoid Robin's eye.

"Who was that so early in the morning?"

"Just a pal," Pauline said casually. "Where was I? Oh, about Calvin—it's no wonder Mother was so wild to get her hooks into him. He must own half the world! Not that you'd know it from talking to him. It was truly embarrassing the way she dragged all the details out of the poor man. He's really the most amusing dinner companion. He's been all over the world and knows all kinds of famous people, but it just comes out naturally in conversation—you know what I mean?"

Yes, I know exactly what you mean, Robin thought bitterly. Who knew better than she how charming he could be when he tried?

"Even Dad thought he was a doll," Pauline continued.

"Papa doesn't like dolls," Dicky protested. "That's sissy. Your old Calvin Carrington sounds like a big dumb sissy," he repeated crossly. Dicky never liked any conversation that didn't revolve around him.

Pauline regarded her brother with the goodwill she seemed to have for the whole human race that morning. "You think so, do you? Suppose I told you he flies his own airplane—what would you say to that?"

The little boy's face lit up like a light bulb. "Really? Truly?" She nodded her head. "Would he give me a ride? Would he, Sis?"

"Well, I don't know about that, but he invited us all to swim in his pool anytime we like. As a matter of fact, a whole group of us are getting together there today. I have a million phone calls to make."

"Can I come too?" Dicky asked, not wanting to be left out.

"I suppose so." Pauline turned to Robin. "It's going to be a reunion. Sally Boswell, my good friend from San Francisco, and two other girls flew in last night and the whole crowd from the ship is coming."

Robin smiled at her friend's animated face. Remembering how that group had partied into the small hours, she decided this was probably the last time she would see Pauline at breakfast. "It sounds like fun," she commented.

"It will be, you'll see. And I want you to get to know"—was it her imagination or did Pauline hesitate for an instant before continuing—"all my friends."

Robin looked at her intently and Pauline dropped her eyes to her plate and started eating rapidly. "I want you to get to know . . . " Who? Robin wondered?

From the other girl's suppressed excitement, it didn't take much insight to realize she had been about to mention someone special. Robin's heart sank. It wasn't hard to guess who that someone was. Who could resist the rapacious Calvin Carrington when he turned on the charm and decided to add one more scalp to his belt?

As if to confirm her suspicions, Pauline said, "You were such a stick-in-the-mud aboard ship—you were almost as bad as Calvin about not putting in an appearance. But isn't it marvelous that Mother refused to take no for an answer? This vacation is going to be a blast. Did I tell you he has *two* speedboats?" She laughed a little self-consciously. "I'm beginning to sound like Mother and I don't mean to. I'd like Cal if he didn't have a button. He's really a great person."

Robin glanced out the window at a ship on the edge of the horizon. It brought back that magic night before the cruise ended—and her dreams along with it. Yes, it was easy to understand how Pauline had fallen in love so quickly. She only hoped her friend wouldn't be hurt the same way.

Dicky was tugging at her arm. "Can I go too?" he begged, and Robin realized she hadn't been listening. "Pauli's friends are going waterskiing and I want to go with them."

"I'm afraid not," she told him, "I don't know how to water-ski myself, so I couldn't take care of you."

"Not to worry," Pauline told her. "We'll all take turns watching Dicky and I'll teach you how to ski. Remember how fast you picked up surfing? Calvin will help too, I'm sure. He's a natural-born athlete—you can tell just by looking at him."

And that's about the only thing you can tell, Robin thought bitterly. She wished there was some way to warn Pauline, knowing all the while that she would never listen. But maybe he would play fair with her—maybe she wasn't just . . . a diversion. Looking at her friend's shining face, Robin felt that it was more than possible he would return her love. Pushing her chair back abruptly, she said, "If you'll excuse us, Dicky and I have a date on the beach to build a sand castle."

"Okay, you go ahead, I'm going to get on the phone." As Robin started out the door, Pauline added, "Be ready about one o'clock."

"I'll see," Robin answered, and escaped through the wide glass doors before Pauline could insist.

It was almost noon when Mrs. Dahlgren appeared on the patio to check on them. She was dressed to go out and waved them in from the beach so she wouldn't get sand in her fashionable high-heeled shoes. Robin immediately took Dicky's hand and ran thankfully toward the house.

For at least half an hour there had been activity around the Carrington place next door. Servants kept going in and out, setting the patio tables for lunch and starting a charcoal fire in a huge cylindrical barbecue. Robin was an unwilling witness, but Dicky had resisted all her efforts to go elsewhere to play.

"Would you please give Dicky a quick bath and get him dressed," his mother requested. "I'm going to take him with me. My friends, the Engels, from Santa Barbara just rang up and invited us to lunch. They've taken a house here for the season and I thought Dicky would enjoy spending the afternoon with their children."

"Oh, boy!" Dicky shouted. Hawaii was turning out to be his birthday and Christmas all rolled into one.

"It will give you some time to yourself too, dear," Mrs. Dahlgren said kindly. "Why don't you join the young people at Mr. Carrington's? Pauline told me all her friends are going and it will be nice for you to be with people your own age too."

"Thank you, but I . . . uh . . . I have a few things to do."

"Well, suit yourself." The older woman shrugged. "You decide when you want some time off, and would you please have Dicky ready as soon as possible?"

After they had gone, Robin took a tall glass of iced tea and sank gratefully down on an outdoor chaise. Dicky was always a handful when he was excited, which seemed to be his permanent state, and he often left her feeling breathless.

As she leafed idly through a magazine, the sound of rock music came drifting through the tall hedge, disturbing her with reminders. The high, bubbling laughter of girls, mixed with deeper male voices, signaled that the get-together had started next door. After trying unsuccessfully to ignore it, she got up and went indoors, but that didn't help either. The house was too quiet. Then the telephone rang.

Robin knew just as surely as if she could see the person on the other end that it was Pauline telling her to hurry over. Grabbing her purse, she fled out the door while the phone shrilled a summons she was unwilling to answer.

That was to set the pattern of days to come. Robin was either evasive or she slipped away unnoticed, and finally Pauline became exasperated with her. "I don't know what's the matter with you. Even Calvin noticed you never join us. He commented on it today."

Robin's heart caught in her throat. "He did?"

"Yes. None of us can understand what you do with yourself." An idea occurred to her. "You're not staying away because you think you won't know anybody there, are you? That's nonsense, of course, but if that's the reason, it isn't a valid one. Some of the people from the ship are absolute regulars, so, you see, you wouldn't be an outsider, if that is what's worrying you. You remember Tom Manning and Michael Browning, don't you?"

"I remember Michael. Wasn't he the one you spent so much time with?"

"All of us got to be great pals," Pauline remarked casually. "The ship is in port this week and most of the crew hang out at Calvin's."

To her great shame, Robin already knew that. Hating herself but unable to resist, she had peeked through the hedge and watched the partying around the pool. It became increasingly difficult to explain why she was avoiding them, but Robin's days fell into a routine. She took Dicky down to the beach early every morning while the household slept, which they could never understand. Sleeping was a great waste of time as far as both of them were concerned—Hawaiian mornings were too good to miss. The sun reflected off sapphire water trimmed with foamy whitecaps and the sand was strewn with exotic seashells and even an occasional prize—a brilliant-colored glass float detached from some fisherman's net in far-off Japan. They had the beach to themselves in the early hours and splashed around happily in the warm ocean. It was a peaceful time—an interlude before the problems of the day intruded.

One morning Robin and Dicky were doing their usual beachcombing. Heads down and hunched over, they inspected the golden sands for treasure.

"I found one! Come here quick!" The little boy's lilting tones summoned her.

She straightened up just as a deep male voice said, "I'll say you did. That's a beauty," and found herself face to face with Calvin Carrington. It was so unexpected that Robin felt like someone had thrown a beach ball directly at her middle. "Hello. We meet again," he said, smiling urbanely at her, while all she could do was stand there staring at him like an awkward schoolgirl.

Dicky tugged on Robin's arm. "Is that him?" Shading his eyes, he looked at the man towering above him and asked, "Are you the man with the airplane?"

Calvin hunkered down on his heels so he would be at the child's level. "I guess I'm the one."

"Would you take me for a ride?" Dicky asked, coming right to the point.

"Dicky!" Robin gasped. "You shouldn't ask a thing like that." But Calvin merely looked amused.

"Well, I'll tell you—it would be a little difficult because my plane's not here right now," he told the boy.

"Where is it?"

"It's off in the Middle East somewhere, carrying a couple of vice-presidents to a policy meeting on oil," Calvin explained, smiling at the earnest little face.

That didn't make sense to Dicky and he looked to Robin for clarification. "I guess that means the answer is no," she told him.

"Would you settle for a speedboat ride instead?" Calvin asked.

"Oh, boy, you mean it?" When Calvin nodded his

head, Dicky let out a whoop and started to run in an erratic course down the beach, steering an imaginary motorboat and calling out to a flock of startled sea gulls, "I'm going for a ride. Look at me!"

They watched indulgently. "It doesn't take much to make you happy when you're that young," Calvin remarked, and Robin silently agreed, wishing she could go back to that joyful time. "I'm glad I ran into you this morning," he continued. "Besides brightening Dicky's whole day, I satisfied my curiosity about something."

"What's that?"

"I found out you really do exist. For a time there I thought perhaps I had only dreamed you up."

"I'm sure it was a bad dream," she said coldly.

He looked at her intently. "Was that what it was for you?"

Her eyes fell before his penetrating gaze, but she managed to say, "It certainly turned out to be."

He frowned. "Robin, why do you persist in acting like a child? I'll admit we got off on the wrong foot, but why can't you just forget it happened?"

The only emotion he displayed was irritation, and his words, uttered in that curt tone, stung like a whiplash. Well, what did she expect? Any lingering hope she might have cherished that he cared even a little bit was dashed by his casual advice to forget the whole thing. Did forgetting include that lingering kiss at her cabin door? Or the way he held her in his arms on the beach? It obviously did for him. She was furious with herself because she remembered all of it. Even now, his nearness made her legs tremble, but at least she could keep him from knowing. Tossing her head, she said, "Consider it forgotten."

He studied her face and then shook his head. "I don't

think it is, but I've explained the circumstances and given as much of an apology as I intend to. If you expect me to get down on my knees, you're going to be disappointed."

"I would never expect Calvin the Great to do anything so undignified, especially in the bright sunshine," she told him. "Taking advantage of unsuspecting girls in the moonlight is more your line of work, isn't it?"

His face darkened and he clenched his fists. "What makes you think the time of day has anything to do with it? If I wanted to take advantage of you I would do it right here and now," he said contemptuously.

Robin took an involuntary step backward, a little frightened at the fury she had evoked but determined to stand up to him. "And what would that prove? Merely that you're stronger than I."

His expression changed as he deliberately looked her up and down—undressing her with his eyes, Robin thought indignantly. Instinctively she poised for flight but he made no move to touch her. "You might be surprised at what it would prove," he said softly.

She swallowed an angry reply as Dicky appeared and looked pleadingly at Calvin. "Can we go for a ride now?"

Calvin's ill temper dissipated entirely when he turned to the little boy. Smiling indulgently, he said, "How would it be if we swam out to the float instead?"

The raft was used for diving, and though it was anchored only a short way out, the water fell off steeply at that point. Dicky had been deviling Robin for days to take him there, but she always refused. Although she was an excellent swimmer, she considered the responsibility too great.

"Oh, yes, I want to go! Robin says it's too far, even if I wear my life preserver. She says it isn't safe, but she's wrong, isn't she?"

Calvin looked ironically at Robin. "You play everything safe, don't you? Haven't you ever taken a chance on anything?"

Robin knew perfectly well what he meant, but she chose to interpret it literally. "Not with Dicky."

"What's your own excuse?" he asked softly.

Her temper snapped. "I don't wish to discuss it any further. Dicky is my responsibility and I say he can't go."

Very deliberately, he picked up a small blue-and-yellow life preserver lying on the sand. Slipping it over the little boy's head, he hoisted the child onto his back, looking arrogantly at Robin all the while. "And I say he can. How are you going to stop me?" She gritted her teeth in impotent fury, knowing he was too strong for her in every way. As he padded into the water, Calvin said over his shoulder, "You can come too, if you want."

There was nothing to do but follow them, and when Calvin struck out she could see that he was a superb swimmer. At least there was no danger, although that didn't excuse his high-handedness. She swam after them, determined to keep an eye on Dicky in spite of the fact that he was obviously in good hands.

Calvin reached the raft without even breathing hard. After depositing the little boy on the rough rope surface, he hoisted himself up and turned to give Robin a hand, but she spurned his help. "I can manage by myself," she said, scrambling up quickly.

He shrugged, completely disinterested. "Suit yourself."

Dicky ran around inspecting every inch of the flat surface as if he were an archaeologist unearthing rare treasures. After satisfying his curiosity about this forbidden territory, he plopped down on his stomach and peered into the ocean depths. Robin, ashamed that she was panting slightly from the swim, sat on the edge and dangled her legs over the side. But when Calvin sat down next to her, she started to get up.

He frowned and put his arm around her, restraining her easily. "Will you please stay put for a minute? It's like trying to carry on a conversation with a Mexican jumping bean."

"We have nothing to talk about," she said, struggling against his encircling embrace. "You deliberately undermined my authority. I told Dicky he couldn't come out here and you brought him. How do you think I'll get him to listen to me after this?"

"Is that what is really bothering you?"

"I don't know what you mean. And would you please take your hands off me." She willed herself not to think about the last time she was this close to him—the way he held her in his arms and what ecstasy it had been before the bubble burst.

Calvin raised one eyebrow and regarded her quizzically. "I believe you're afraid of me."

"That's ridiculous," she cried, making a move to stand up.

"Will you kindly sit still?" His voice tinged with impatience. "What do you suppose I'm going to do to you out here in full view of the entire population of Honolulu?" Without waiting for a reply, he continued, "Or maybe you're afraid of yourself."

"What is that supposed to mean?"

He ran his finger lightly down her tilted nose and

Robin jerked away angrily. "I think you would like me to kiss you and you're afraid to admit it to yourself."

Her cheeks flamed and this time she jumped quickly to her feet before he could stop her. The nerve of this arrogant man! It was as though he were reading her mind, but the fact that she was picturing the last time they were together didn't mean she wanted to repeat the experience! "Oh . . . you . . . you're impossible," she sputtered. Forgetting completely about Dicky, Robin prepared to dive off the float—her one purpose in life to get away from this terrible man.

Moving almost lazily, his hand shot out and encircled her slim ankle. "I can tell by your face that I'm right. But it isn't any crime, you know, for a pretty girl to want to be kissed in broad daylight, no matter what you think."

"I'll tell you what I think," Robin flared. "I think you're the most conceited man I've ever met. Just because a lot of girls chase after you doesn't mean that every one of them finds you irresistible. I, for one, would be very happy if I never saw you again."

Her breath caught in something like a sob and Calvin regarded her indolently, although something sparked deep in his eyes. Far from being angry at her outburst, he seemed almost pleased. "I'm glad you admit you feel some emotion toward me. It's a step in the right direction."

"You and I are going in totally different directions," she assured him. "I thought I'd made it perfectly clear that I intend to avoid you like a case of the measles."

"Which brings up the next point I want to talk to you about," he said. "Just because I'm not your favorite person doesn't mean you have to sulk in a corner like a bad little girl. The kids are having a great time at my place and they'd like you to join them. Unless you don't trust yourself around me." He gave her a wicked grin.

"That's too silly to deserve an answer," she replied with a withering glance.

"Then why don't you prove it?"

"*Some* of us have to work for a living," she told him. "I'm not over here strictly on vacation like the rest of you."

"Oh, poor baby," he said with exaggerated but false sympathy in his voice.

Even to her own ears Robin sounded slightly pompous, and it didn't endear him to her any further to have him catch her up on it. "What difference does it make whether I'm there or not?" she cried.

"It doesn't make the slightest difference to me, but for some strange reason it does to Pauline. She's gotten it into her head that she hurt your feelings in some way."

"But that's crazy—Pauline is my best friend."

"She's fond of you too and that's what bothers her—the fact that she might have slighted you somehow. She's a good kid." His voice softened as he talked about her and Robin realized unhappily that her surmise was correct. Calvin was falling in love.

I'm really happy for her, Robin told herself. Pauline was a changed person these last few days. One would have to be blind not to see that she was in love too. It was nice that Calvin returned her affections instead of treating her like he treated all the other unfortunate girls who loved him. And why shouldn't he be drawn to Pauline? They were perfect for each other—both so charming and handsome—and, of course, rich. Someone like Robin could never hope to enter their charmed circle. Not that she wanted to, but it was now obvious that he was strictly off limits.

She bent her head so he couldn't see her expression and said in a husky little voice, "I would never do anything to hurt Pauline." Had she glanced up, she would have been puzzled by the look on Calvin's face.

"Hey, come here, quick, there's a fish—and there's another and another." Dicky's excited voice interrupted them.

Calvin went over to lie face down on the raft next to him. "By golly, you're right. There's a whole school of them, in fact."

"They're all yellow with black stripes. And look over there at those little bitty ones. They got a spot and a black line—I can see their insides."

"Those small ones are neon tetras," Calvin said, putting his arm around the little boy's shoulders. "Those are very common—you'll see a lot of them. But take a look at that one with a spot on its face swimming kind of sideways. That's called a clown fish. Can you tell why?" He patiently pointed out the different varieties, explaining everything in simple language so the child could understand.

Robin watched them, bemused. Would she ever understand this strange man? He was sarcastic and biting one moment, playing the male game of trying to force her to admit her true feelings while he just stood back and smiled smugly. But the next minute he was all tenderness and patience toward a small boy who might have been considered a nuisance by some men. Who was the real Calvin Carrington? Would she ever know? Probably not, since he belonged to Pauline. Let her sort it out—she was more than a match for him anyway.

Pauline always knew the right thing to say and do—obviously, from the look on his face when he mentioned her name.

"Robin, come look at the fish." Dicky summoned her. She dutifully joined them and stood peering into the sparkling water. "Tell her about that one," he said, pointing.

But Calvin leaned back on one elbow, inspecting her insolently over every part of her anatomy. She was painfully aware of the briefness of her bikini and knew he was enjoying her embarrassment. Would he dare say something outrageous in front of the child? But Calvin merely remarked, "It's hard to tell Robin anything."

Completely unaware of the undercurrent between the two adults, Dicky sat crosslegged on the raft. "I wish I could catch some."

"What would you do with them?" Calvin asked.

"I'd put them in a jar and keep them in my room."

"Do you think they'd like that?" Calvin asked. "They have a whole ocean to swim around in now."

Dicky thought about this solemnly and Robin realized it was perhaps the first time he had considered anything but his own desires. In a completely nonjudgmental way, Calvin had pointed out that other things have feelings too. Again she wondered at the perception of this contradictory man. Dicky made his decision. "No, I guess they wouldn't like it. But I want to watch them some more. Will you bring me out here again?" he asked Calvin.

"You bet," Calvin said approvingly, "and I'll take you on that speedboat ride I promised too."

"When?" Dicky asked, reminded of the treat in store. "Can Robin come too? When can we go?"

"How about this afternoon—is that soon enough?"

"Yippee!"

"Hey, wait a minute," Robin protested, "I'd have to ask his mother first. You really shouldn't get him all excited until we get permission."

For once Calvin agreed with her. "Robin is right."

"She'll say yes." Dicky was already struggling into his life preserver. "Let's go ask her right now."

The two adults looked at each other and laughed, the tension between them broken for the moment by the small boy's enthusiasm.

Chapter Four

Robin stood in front of the mirror trying to pin her hair on top of her head, but the shining strands kept slipping through her nervous fingers and she gave an exclamation of annoyance. Pauline, lounging in the doorway, watched approvingly.

"I can't tell you how happy I am that you're finally joining us," Pauline said. "I was beginning to think I had done something to hurt your feelings."

Dicky was hopping impatiently up and down on the patio outside and Robin stuck a final bobby pin in the shining curls, tightened the straps on her yellow bikini, and turned to face the other girl. No point in telling her she was only going along because there was no way out of it this time. Linking arms, she said warmly, "Don't be silly—you could never do anything to hurt anyone." And it was true.

Pauline was genuinely nice, and it wasn't her fault

that they loved the same man. She couldn't help it if Calvin preferred her, and she had no idea how Robin felt. It would make her miserable, and what good would it do anyway? You can't make one person love another—it's all a matter of chemistry, they say. But at least Robin could hide her feelings. That much she could do for her friend.

Arm in arm, they went downstairs, a sight to gladden any man's eyes—Pauline, slim and dark, a perfect foil for the golden Robin.

Mrs. Dahlgren was waiting for them at the foot of the stairs with some last-minute admonitions. She heartily approved of any outing that involved her illustrious neighbor, but at the same time she had some apprehensions about the exuberant Dicky. "You will watch him carefully, won't you, Robin? And you too, Pauline. You know how wiggly that child can be, and he simply doesn't know the meaning of the word *fear*. Do be sure that he wears his life preserver at all times."

"Don't worry, Mother, every one of us will keep an eye on him."

Mrs. Dahlgren sighed. "I know, but I can't help worrying. He's such an *active* youngster. You were a perfect little lady at his age. I wonder if I'll ever get used to a small boy."

"He will be in the boat with Cal," Pauline told her soothingly, "and I guarantee nothing will happen to him."

Mention of their neighbor's name had the usual result. "It was so nice of Calvin to be bothered with Dicky. I just can't get over what a charming *gentleman* he is," Mrs. Dahlgren enthused. "And so hospitable, having you young people over all the time. I never even see you anymore. Not that I'm complaining," she hastily added. Mrs. Dahlgren was so delighted at the way things were progressing between Pauline and Calvin that she hadn't nagged about anything for days.

"Aren't you *ever* coming?" Dicky's complaining voice called from the patio. "They're gonna go without us if you don't hurry."

A whole group of young people were milling around on the beach by the time they got there and two motor launches bobbed offshore. The sand was littered with so many water skis that it looked like there had been a shipwreck.

Some of the group were already putting on the shining slivers of wood and others were just standing around laughing and joking. The sun shone down on glistening, lithe bodies.

"Listen, everybody!" Pauline commanded their attention. "I want you to meet Robin." A hail of warm welcome greeted the newcomer and Pauline continued, "She's never skied before, so we're going to need some volunteers."

This request was promptly answered by all the young men present, and Robin hurriedly said, "Please don't worry about me. I have to watch Dicky anyway, so you go ahead and I'll just come along for the ride."

"Nonsense, we'll all keep an eye on Dicky. You're here to have fun like the rest of us," Pauline told her.

"Sure, we'll show you the ropes—there's nothing to it," one of the men told her confidently.

Robin eyed the water skis dubiously. "I was always taught that walking on the water was a miracle."

"It isn't a whole lot harder than surfing," Pauline scoffed, "and you learned how to do that, didn't you?"

"Why do I have the feeling this isn't as easy as you're

trying to make out?" Robin asked, and was greeted by a storm of reassurances coupled with conflicting bits of advice. In the midst of the bedlam, Calvin appeared.

"Is everybody ready?" he asked.

A chorus of voices greeted him. "Ready and waiting." . . . "How do you want us to divide up?"

"To start with, Michael will drive one boat and I'll drive the other. Decide among yourselves who's going to go first. The rest of you hightail it out to the raft and wait your turn. I'll take Dicky with me." He barked out instructions like a man used to giving orders and having them obeyed.

Robin waited uncertainly while he scooped up the little boy and started wading out to the launch. No mention had been made of her specifically and, in fact, Calvin had barely glanced at her. After an indecisive moment, she started after them.

He turned and noticed her, seemingly for the first time. "Are you gracing us with your presence, Miss O'Neill? Surely you must prefer the other boat with handsome young Mike at the wheel."

"I'm afraid I have no choice, *Mr.* Carrington. I'm Dicky's governess, or had you forgotten?" she asked sweetly. "Whither he goeth and all that sort of thing."

He smiled back mockingly. "I quite understand and I'll try to make it as painless for you as possible. I'll pretend you're not here."

Robin glared at him, but before she could answer Dicky interrupted. "I want to water-ski too. Can't I, Mr. Carrington? Please!"

"Well, it's like this, sport. We don't happen to have any skis your size today, but tell you what—I'll get you some the next time, how's that?"

After being assured that no, he couldn't wear adult skis, Dicky had to content himself with future promises.

Calvin plunked the child in the middle next to the steering wheel and Robin climbed lightly onto the wide leather seat on the other side of him. With a great roar, the powerful boat took off. Dicky was fascinated as the prow rose out of the water and his chortles brought a smile to their faces. Glancing back over the churning wake, Robin was amazed to see that they were towing Pauline's friend, Sally. As she watched, the girl rose out of the water and stood erect, leaning far back, her outstretched arms holding the ropes tightly. It was an enchanting sight, as though a mermaid had risen from the waves.

"How did she do that?" Robin shouted above the noise of the engine?

"What? I can't hear you," Calvin shouted back.

She got on her knees and leaned over Dicky, putting her mouth close to Calvin's ear so he could hear her. "How did she just rise up out of the water that way? I thought they had to start from the float."

He turned his head and their faces were so close that his lips brushed hers and she could taste the salt on them. She drew in her breath sharply. Did he think she had planned it?

He smiled at her and said, "That was very nice."

As she started to draw back, he put his right arm around her shoulders, bringing her close again while he steered with the other hand. "What did you say?"

Robin was uncomfortably aware of the warmth of his lean, muscular body as he held her near. But to make a fuss with Dicky sandwiched between them was unwise. You could never count on Calvin to play by the rules.

She cupped her hand over his ear, making sure that he wouldn't catch her unawares a second time. "I said, doesn't the boat have to pull them off a flat surface like the raft?"

They were approaching it and he held up his hand, telling her to wait. As he swung the boat in an arc, Sally let go of the rope and glided effortlessly onto the float. Calvin cut the motor, and as they waited for the next skier to get in position, he answered her question.

"If you're a beginner it's better to start from a hard surface. We'll do that with you. But these kids are real water babies. They've been skiing all their lives and they can get up from a puddle if they want."

As they were talking, the young people milled around on the raft and soon another one was ready to take off. Calvin gunned the boat and they started again, towing one of the men this time, an expert skier who performed intricate maneuvers for an appreciative audience, especially Robin and Dicky. Pauline took the next turn, and for the first time Dicky was properly impressed by his big sister. They watched, enthralled, as one person after another lined up for a chance to skim over the water, and the afternoon flew by.

After they circled around until everybody had at least one turn, Calvin said, "I think they've all had a go at it—now it's time for your first lesson."

Robin was having second thoughts because, although they made it look simple, she knew deep down that it was more complicated than it seemed. "I think maybe I'll skip it this time." She demurred, but Calvin wasn't having any.

"I'm going to dock at the float so you can hop out. The kids will put your skis on. It isn't easy the first few times but you'll get the hang of it. Just grab hold of the ropes and lean back. The momentum will tighten the lines and you'll flit over the water like a bird."

Despite his casual assurances, Robin had definite apprehensions. But she didn't want him to know she was afraid, so when he passed by the raft, she did as she was told.

It's like a pit stop at an auto race, she thought. Everyone rushed forward to get ready, urging her on and giving instructions. Before she knew it, she was standing at the edge with two terribly awkward slats fastened to her feet. Conflicting bits of advice were flying around as each one gave a different version of the right way for a beginner to learn. Poor Robin was confused, to say the least, but game to the end.

It was only when they slipped a life preserver over her head that she protested. "I don't need that—I can swim."

"It's no reflection on you," Pauline soothed. "Everyone has to wear one for safety reasons."

"I don't need it," Robin insisted, thinking they were trying to baby her.

"Yes, you do. Calvin gave us strict instructions that you should wear one and you don't argue with him. Now get set—he's going to be around in a minute."

How did I get myself into this mess, Robin wondered, but that was her last coherent thought for some time to come. As the boat made a pass, helpful hands guided her in the right direction. She seized the handle, glided off the float—and promptly sank like a stone. As she surfaced, spluttering and gasping, Calvin drove off in a wide circle. Several of the onlookers jumped in the water, hoisting her back on the raft and shouting encouragement.

"That's okay, Robin—it happens to all of us." . . . "Sure, you'll catch on." . . . "Don't give up—it gets worse."

Again Calvin brought the boat around and again she caught the handle and slid off only to sink once more, as ignominiously as the time before. Then the whole laborious process started all over. The boat veered off, she was fished out of the water, skis akimbo, and guided back into position by determined tutors. Only once did she almost succeed. For a fraction of a second she crouched, half in and half out of the water, but the moment of triumph was short lived. A playful wave slapped her down and the rope slipped from her numb fingers.

Robin didn't know how many times she went through this torture. But each time she clenched her teeth and came gasping to the surface, determined to try again if it killed her, which she decided it probably would.

Finally, Calvin brought the boat alongside and killed the motor. "I think it's time for a rest," he said.

Robin dashed the water out of her eyes and said grimly, "No, keep going. I'll try some more."

He looked at her and grinned. "I think you've had enough for a while."

She tried to straighten her back and winced with the effort. Not only that—her arms felt like they had been jerked out of their sockets and stuck back in. Her legs, too, were trembling from exertion, but there was no way she was going to let him know it. Lifting her chin gallantly, she said, "Start the motor, I'm ready to go again."

Instead, he climbed out of the launch and said, "Here, Tom, you take it for a while." Putting his arm around Robin, he led her away from the edge, saying, "Come on, little one, I think you need a rest."

"I'm fine." She resisted bravely, actually wanting nothing more than to be cuddled in his arms like a tired child..

Gently, he brushed the wet hair out of her eyes and said, "You don't have to prove you're a good sport—we already know that. But if you keep on gulping seawater there won't be any left for the rest of us. Come on, lie down for a while."

Gratefully, she stretched out on her back, oblivious to the rough matting. It was blissful just to lie completely still. When she heard a girl's voice warning Dicky not to take off his life preserver and heard his response, Robin relaxed completely. He was being taken care of and pretty soon she would go to him, but right now she needed to rest for a minute.

The voices all around her seemed to come from a great distance. Two people were arguing the relative merits of different kinds of surfboards and Michael and Pauline were discussing a new nightclub. They were talking very softly but Robin caught the words *Flaming Torch* and *dancing*. Evidently the group was planning a night on the town.

The sun shone down and warmed her aching body, making dancing spots under her closed eyelids. The voices receded further and she almost dozed off, but when a shadow passed over her face, she looked up to see Calvin lying on his side next to her, his head propped on one hand.

He was looking searchingly at her, and for once the mocking light was absent from his dark eyes. "Are you all right?"

She started to get up, but he put his hand on her

shoulder and gently pushed her back. "No, lie still for a bit."

"I'm fine, really." But she lay back, basking in his nearness.

His hand rested on her shoulder for a moment and then he reached up and smoothed her eyebrows with one forefinger. Gently he traced the curve of her cheek before cupping her chin in his palm. "Such a little one to have so much spirit," he murmured.

Robin smiled. "Nobody likes a cream puff."

"Don't jump to conclusions," he said. "I happen to have a pronounced sweet tooth."

She lowered her lashes and, ignoring his words, said, "I really must have looked like a jerk out there."

"Nonsense. Everybody has to start somewhere." Waving his arm, he said, "Do you think they were born knowing how to ski? They took their share of dunkings, but the difference is they learned when they were kids and didn't care about dignity."

Robin sat up abruptly, eyes widening in horror. "Kids—Dicky! Good Lord, where is he?" She realized it had been some time since she had heard his voice.

"Relax—he's fine and having the time of his life. *Everyone* is looking out for him."

"But I'm responsible for him. I promised I'd watch him every minute." She tried to get to her feet and winced as sore muscles protested.

"Look, there he is now," Calvin told her.

The speedboat shot by and Robin caught a glimpse of Dicky kneeling on the wide seat, hanging on for dear life and shouting encouragement to the girl strung out astern. His hair was plastered down and his eyes sparkled.

Robin smiled. "He won't have any trouble sleeping

tonight. When he comes down to earth, the problem will be keeping him awake long enough to stuff him into his pajamas. Maybe he's had enough for today."

"Don't spoil his fun. He's in better shape than you are right now."

Calvin reached down to help her up, but instead of giving her a hand, he put his arms under hers and pulled her swiftly to her feet. Caught off balance, Robin lurched against him, and his arms enfolded her to keep her from falling.

Her body was molded to his and she was acutely conscious of the fact that only a couple of tiny scraps of cloth separated them. She could feel how muscular he was under the smooth skin. Suddenly it was difficult to breathe and she could feel her breast rising and falling with the effort. They stood that way for only a moment—not long enough for anyone else to notice, but Robin turned red as a rose.

Calvin looked at her in amusement. "You must be the only girl left in the world who knows how to blush. I wasn't sure it could still be done."

Robin was furious with herself. Why was she cursed with this fair skin that betrayed her every emotion? "I'm not blushing," she said. "It's the sun. I'm getting sunburned."

"Of course you are," he assured her gravely.

"Hey, Cal, do you want to take her around for a while? I'd kind of like to have a turn now." Tom climbed up next to them, a blessed interruption in Robin's eyes.

"Sure, Tom, get your skis on," Calvin said. "Come on, Robin, we'll go for a ride. Unless you think you'd like to try again."

"No thanks—I couldn't swallow another drop," she laughed.

"Okay, we'll save it till next time then."

She was filled with a warmth that had nothing to do with the sun. His casual assumption that there was going to be a next time filled her with almost suffocating happiness. The chance of being beside him, having him take her hand in his if only to steady her, made her forget the promise she'd made to avoid him. Robin knew deep down that she was being foolish, probably even heading for a fall, but she couldn't help it. He was so gentle with her today. This golden afternoon would live forever no matter what came after. She would always keep the memory of his hard body pressed against hers, the two of them melting together like one person.

"Robin, will you hurry up?" Dicky complained and she jumped guiltily.

"Are you sure you haven't had enough?" she asked, scanning his face anxiously. "I think it's about time to go in."

"No, no, not yet," he pleaded.

"Well, all right, just a little while more. But only if you promise to go to bed tonight with no arguments, okay?"

Dicky nodded happily, secure in the knowledge that he could twist Robin around his little finger any day in the week.

"About tonight," Calvin said, "since the champ here is going to be grounded early, how would you like to have dinner with me?"

Robin was caught unawares by the unexpected invitation, but since he started up the motor and couldn't hear her anyway, she was spared an immediate answer.

"You can tell me later," he hollered over the din.

Her head was spinning with more than the motion of the boat! What should she say? What about Pauline? One part of her mentioned that old saw about all being fair in love and war, but Robin rejected the notion. Maybe other girls played by those rules but she didn't. There was no way she could betray a friend and live with herself. There were other reasons, too, for not going out with him. Who knew better than she what pain this fickle man was capable of inflicting? Calvin was a playboy—all girls were fair game to him and anyone with good sense would stay away from him completely. Even Pauline, if she only knew it. But she obviously wanted him, so it came back to the question, Was it fair for Robin to accept his invitation? On the other hand, Pauline had already made plans for the evening with Michael and the others. For some reason they hadn't included Calvin, so she wasn't really depriving her of anything. Besides, it was just dinner and she was making far too much of it. And yet . . .

Robin was still torn with indecision when Calvin finally decreed that it was time to go in. As the boat neared shore, she honestly didn't know what her answer was going to be.

"So—what time shall I pick you up and where would you like to dine?" he asked when the noise of the motor died and she could hear him.

"I'm not sure . . ." she started uncertainly, meaning, of course, that she hadn't made up her mind to go. But he chose to use his own interpretation.

"All right, then, I'll set the time. Pick you up at seven o'clock."

"Wait, I . . ." Her protest went unfinished as Calvin turned on his heel and strode down the beach to supervise the stowing of the gear.

"Robin, I'm tired. Will you carry me?" Dicky tugged at her arm and she looked down at a very weary little boy. The excitement that had buoyed him up all day was spent and he flopped down like a deflated balloon.

"Of course I will, honey lamb. Here, climb on my back," and she knelt on the sand next to him.

"Wait, Robin, he's too heavy. I'll carry him up to the house for you."

The offer came from Michael Browning, but Pauline, who was standing beside him, put her hand on his arm and said warningly, "No, you'd better not. Mother will be waiting."

A meaningful glance passed between them and he reluctantly said, "I guess you're right."

That seemed strange. What difference did it make that Mrs. Dahlgren was waiting? She wouldn't blame Michael because they were late. She hardly knew him except from the ship and probably didn't even know he was still in town. Robin shrugged. Well, no matter, it wasn't really important—and she dismissed it from her mind.

"I'll help," Pauline said, and the two of them made a basket with their clasped hands and carried the little boy up to the house.

Mrs. Dahlgren was indeed waiting for them and clucking about the hour. "I had no idea you would be gone so long. Do you know what time it is?"

Dicky revived long enough to tell his mother, "We had lots of fun. And you know what? Mr. Carrington says that next time he's going to get me a pair of water skis and teach me how."

Mrs. Dahlgren beamed, instantly diverted from her bad mood. Any mention of Calvin's name produced that reaction and, realizing how her employer would feel about her plans for the evening, Robin suffered a momentary guilt pang.

"We didn't know it was getting so late," she apologized.

"That's all right, dear, I knew you were in good hands," Mrs. Dahlgren smiled. "But I had visions of the three of you coming to the table in your bathing suits. You'd better hurry now—you barely have time to get cleaned up before dinner."

It was now or never and very tentatively, Robin said, "Uh . . . I won't be here for dinner this evening."

Mrs. Dahlgren looked at her in surprise. "Where are you going?"

Without answering directly, Robin replied, "You said I could have a night off when I wanted, and if it's all right with you I'll take tonight."

"Well, you could have given me a little notice," her employer complained.

"If it's inconvenient for you, I won't go," Robin said hastily. Maybe this was the sign from heaven she had been waiting for.

But Pauline intervened.

"Mother, how could you? Robin hasn't had a night off since we got here. She's certainly entitled to it," Pauline said, making Robin feel just slightly lower than a worm. "And I won't be here for dinner either," she added.

Mrs. Dahlgren was outraged. "You might at least have told me sooner! Where are you girls going?" It was a question Robin had been dreading and she said nothing, waiting for Pauline to disclose her plans. Then maybe Mrs. Dahlgren would assume they were going together. But for once, Pauline was silent, or maybe she just didn't have a chance to get a word in before her mother rushed on, "What am I supposed to tell the cook? She's already prepared dinner and you know how temperamental she is. Honestly, Pauline, sometimes you show absolutely no consideration." Mrs. Dahlgren directed the tirade at her daughter, but Robin knew she was included.

Pauline was cheerfully unrepentant. "You worry too much, Mother. Mrs. Ching is a darling—she won't mind a bit. There will be that many less to clean up after and she will probably be delighted."

"That doesn't excuse your behavior . . ." The sound of Mrs. Dahlgren's voice followed Robin as she made a hasty retreat.

Chapter Five

It was almost seven o'clock and Robin was ready for her date. She stood in front of the mirror, surveying herself anxiously. Was this dress all right? She looked critically at the beige frock printed with tiny white daisies and her delicate brows creased in a frown. The closet was full of lovely gowns donated by a generous Pauline, but Robin felt it wouldn't be right to wear one tonight. This dress had been made for her by Sister Anne, and while the workmanship was impeccable, the style left something to be desired. Unfortunately, the Sisters were as unworldly as they were charitable. Their idea of the proper attire for a young lady was anything that came up to the chin and down to the fingertips.

Robin's eyes narrowed as she picked up a pair of scissors. With decisive snips, she ripped the exquisitely small stiches securing a double row of ruffles. What a difference it made! Underneath all that little-girl frou-

frou was a lovely neckline, uncluttered and pure in design. The curve of her breast was just a subtle hint above the simple oval.

Another few snips and the sleeves lost their superfluous ornamentation. Robin looked at herself with satisfaction. That was better—in fact it was darn good! Maybe that was the secret of high style—you didn't add, you subtracted.

Now she was ready and there was nothing to put off the inevitable. Butterflies were doing a ballet in her midsection and her fingers were cold as ice. This is ridiculous, Robin told herself, it's only a dinner date— it isn't anything special. But she knew she was lying to herself. Calvin made *everything* special.

She picked up her purse and went slowly down the stairs, aware of the fact that she was merely postponing the inevitable explanations. She had managed to evade Mrs. Dahlgren's questions earlier, but they were bound to be repeated unless she could avoid her completely. With a little time, though—maybe by tomorrow a story would occur to her that was satisfying but still basically the truth. A tall order!

And wasn't it strange that Pauline hadn't asked where she was going? For that matter, it was odd that the other girl hadn't mentioned her own plans either. For days Pauline had regaled them all with every detail of her active social life. Or had she? There was something evasive about the way she avoided telling her mother where she was going, just as Robin had done. Was it possible Pauline had a new boyfriend? That would certainly be something she would avoid telling her mother at all costs! But even while it gave her spirits a lift, Robin knew the idea was foolish. Who would want anyone else when they could have Calvin?

Luckily, she didn't meet anyone on the stairs, and the front hall was empty. She opened the big paneled front door as quietly as possible and slipped out, closing it softly behind her. Skirting the dense jungle of foliage that lined the drive, she walked down to the road, hoping to catch Calvin before he drove in. It was a little awkward, but she would just say that, since she was all ready, she decided to stroll out to meet him.

As she reached the street, his car drew up beside her, a long, low foreign one with wire wheels. Wouldn't you know it, Robin thought. His car looks just like him—handsome and dangerous!

He hopped out and came around to open the door for her. "Am I late?"

"No, I was early, and it was such a beautiful night I decided to meet you halfway," she said.

"And about time too," he told her approvingly, meanwhile helping her into the car. "Have I mentioned that you look very beautiful tonight?"

"No, but I was sure you would get around to it."

"You're a conceited little wench," he said severely. "Probably the result of being chased by scores of avid suitors."

That was really funny, thought Robin, especially coming from him!

He covered her hand with his and asked, "Is there anyplace special you would like to dine?"

"No. I really don't know Honolulu at all. Why don't you pick the place?"

"In that case, I have a reservation at the Pialuani." He started the motor and the big car purred into action. "I think you'll like it."

Robin knew she would like a hot dog stand if she

could be with him but she merely commented, "Hawaiian names are so funny."

"I suppose so, but they probably think the same about ours."

"They're so exotic-sounding, though, it's hard to remember this is actually part of the United States."

"The Hawaiians are very proud of their status. The surest way to insult one is to say you're going back to the States," he told her. "The correct way to put it is, 'I'm going back to the mainland.'"

"I'll remember," she promised. "You warned me just in time. I guess we'll be going back to the mainland"—she smiled "in about two weeks."

After an almost imperceptible pause, Calvin asked, "Will you be sorry to leave?"

Robin lowered her head and examined her small hands clasped tightly in her lap. If he only knew! She had been trying to put the thought out of her mind. The prospect of life without Calvin was a desolate one. Even if she could never belong to him, just knowing he was close by made every day exciting. Those chance meetings on the beach, his warm hand holding hers— all those things made the difference between merely existing and living. He wouldn't even remember her name a week after she was gone, but she would think of him always.

Realizing that he was waiting for an answer, Robin said, "Yes, I'll be sorry to leave here. Hawaii is a magic place."

"Like something out of a storybook?" he asked.

"Yes, don't you agree?"

He looked at her intently, then shook his head. "No, my love, I don't agree, but that's because I live in the real world and I'm afraid you live in a fantasy one."

"That's not true," she protested. "I know there are things in life that are disagreeable but I just choose to ignore the unpleasant side."

"That's why you believe in fairy tales," he told her. "Everything turns out all right in the end and the prince wins the princess with one chaste kiss."

"What's wrong with that?"

His lip curled and he said, "I think there was a little more to it than that."

Robin was suddenly uncomfortable. "Well, at least you have to admit it's romantic."

He chuckled and his eyes softened as he looked at her. "Yes, little one, it's very romantic."

The air was balmy and stars were set like gems in a black velvet sky, a fortune of diamonds splashed across the firmament with a lavish hand. Tropical flowers studded the darkness and everyone seemed to be going to a party.

Robin breathed in the sweet-scented air and said, "This place is a paradise—in fact, that's what they should have named it—Paradise Island." Calvin twined his fingers with hers and that was the crowning touch.

All too soon they arrived at their destination, but Robin reminded herself that the evening had just begun. The restaurant was on top of a tall building, and when they were ushered into the dining room she caught her breath. It covered the entire floor and full-length windows presented a view of the city that was unbelievable—a sight to challenge the stars. There was color and movement everywhere. Jewel-toned signs blinked on and off and moving cars made a Morse code of brilliant dashes. Street lamps were strung like diamond necklaces carelessly flung with a profligate hand.

Calvin glanced indulgently at her rapt face. "Is this all right?"

"All right! It's the most beautiful place I've ever seen!"

"I thought you might like it," he said.

The headwaiter bowed and ushered them to a small table by one of the broad windows. Looking directly down, Robin could see things in detail, and she bumped her head against the glass trying to get a better view.

"I don't know if this was such a good choice after all," Calvin laughed. "I have a feeling I'm not going to get much of your attention. I should have picked someplace so dark that I'd be the only attraction."

She was immediately contrite. "I'm sorry. I'm behaving like a country cousin and you must be ashamed of me."

"You know that's not true." He leaned forward and the candle in the middle of the snowy tablecloth made little flames in his eyes. "I wouldn't change a thing about you. You're warm and gentle and completely unspoiled—do you know how rare that is nowadays?"

"You're saying the same thing I said, only in a nicer way." She smiled. "I guess I am unsophisticated but I can't pretend I'm not having a good time when I am."

"That's what makes you so different. Just promise me you'll never change."

Their heads were close together, and although only their eyes touched, she felt as cherished as if he were holding her in his arms.

"Would you care to order some wine, Mr. Carrington?" A waiter stood discreetly by their table and the fragile rapport was shattered.

He handed Calvin the wine list and, after a selection

had been made, Robin said, "I see you're well known here."

He shrugged. "It's their business."

"Do you spend a lot of time in Hawaii? Pauline says you have houses all over the world." Robin could have bitten her tongue for having brought up Pauline's name, but he didn't seem to notice. Or at least he didn't react in any special way.

"I have a few places here and there, but I've been spending quite a bit of time here because we just bought a hotel on the island of Kauai. That's the one they call the Garden Island."

Robin was surprised. "I didn't know you were in the hotel business. I thought you were in oil and cattle ranches and such."

"I'm in any business that makes money. When they don't I dump them."

His face was hawklike and she sensed the ruthlessness that lurked behind that polished exterior. Whether it was a car or a company—or a girl—he got rid of them when they ceased to satisfy. It was a chilling thought, but she refused to dwell on it. Tonight was special and nothing could ruin it.

Resolutely, she asked, "Is it a big hotel like the Royal Hawaiian?"

"Bigger. Actually, it's a self-contained resort. We have a golf course and tennis courts, of course, and three or four swimming pools. This is just the first in a chain we plan to build all over the world." Robin digested this in silence and he said, "Would you like to see it?"

"Oh, yes," she answered, thinking perhaps he had a picture in his pocket.

"Fine, we'll fly over after dinner."

She looked at him in amazement. "Just like that?"

"Sure, why not? It's only about twenty minutes from here."

"I hear it but I don't believe it." She sat back, shaking her head. "I'll never get used to you people who can do whatever you want, whenever you want. I wonder what it's like."

"I'll show you. Tell me where you want to go and I'll take you."

"That's a tall order," she told him. "I haven't been anywhere and I want to go everywhere."

"You might have to tag around after me the rest of your life," he said lightly.

She looked down at the tablecloth and carefully straightened her fork a fraction of an inch. "Tell me more about your hotel," she said, ignoring his remark.

"It would be much easier to show it to you. How about it?"

Knowing how impetuous he could be, Robin was very firm. "I couldn't possibly," she said, forestalling any attempts at persuasion, "but I do want to hear about it."

Over dinner, in answer to her questions, he told her about the proposed chain of resorts that were only a tiny fraction of his far-flung empire. His holdings were so vast and varied that she had trouble even comprehending some of them. And the homes! A villa in Marbella, a town house in New York, an apartment in London, and who knew what else. Robin's spirits started to droop a little as she began to get an insight into the sheer power of this man. He controlled the lives of hundreds of people and could shatter a man's career with one phone call. Looking at his confident face, Robin knew he would do it, too. No wonder he reminded her of a pirate the first time she saw him.

Now at least it was clear why he had never married. Although he could have any woman he wanted, she would have to be somebody special to fit into his world—a way of life that Robin could only dimly imagine—a world of silks and servants and untold wealth. She had known from the first that he was out of reach but she hadn't realized how far. What could a man like that possibly see in a naive girl who bumped her head against the glass trying to look out? That's the story of my life, Robin thought sadly.

But Pauline had a chance. Although she was young, she would make him a good wife. She was chic and clever and had been schooled in all the correct things. Oh, well, it would be nice to keep him in the family, so to speak. Maybe I can baby-sit for their children, Robin thought wryly, but the notion caused an actual pain in her breast and she lowered her face.

"What's the matter, honey?" She glanced up and saw him looking at her gravely. "Is something wrong?" he asked.

She forced a smile. "No. I'm just a little tired, I guess. It's been a long, eventful day."

"Right. I'll get the check." And he gestured to the waiter.

When they were in the car once more, she started to thank him for the lovely evening.

"Would you like to finish up with a nightcap at my place?" he asked casually.

Robin sat up a little straighter. All the warnings she had been given about what to do when a man asked you to his apartment surfaced. The proper answer of course was a firm no, but he was being so kind for once that she hated to spoil things. If she declined, would that bring the mocking smile to his mouth that she so dreaded? It was all very well for him to say he preferred an unspoiled girl; it was quite another for her to act like a frightened maiden defending her virtue. Which he hasn't asked for, Robin reminded herself honestly. But still, it probably wasn't a good idea. It was almost midnight and it might look . . . well, funny.

"It isn't out of the way. We're neighbors, remember?" he said.

"I really don't think . . ." she started uncertainly.

"Are you afraid I'm going to overpower you and carry you off to my circular bed complete with built-in stereo?" She couldn't see his face but she could tell he was laughing at her again.

"Don't be silly," she snapped, knowing her cheeks were pink and grateful that he couldn't see them.

"Then it's all settled. We'll have one drink at my house and then I'll take you home like a perfect gentleman. Unless you don't want me to," he added.

He was a most infuriating man! Lifting her chin and using what she hoped was a very sophisticated voice, she said, "I think it would be quite amusing to have a drink at your place."

He sounded like he was choking but managed to turn it into a cough. In a voice strangled with merriment he said, "I'll try my best to make it . . . amusing."

Robin had always secretly wanted to see Calvin's house. Pauline had raved about it and it turned out to be everything she had said it was. Houses take on the character of their owners and there was no doubt about the kind of man who lived in this one. It was rich and masculine, opulent but in an understated way. The

living room had deep comfortable chairs in a warm
tobacco brown and the beige carpeting was deep piled.
Softly shaded lamps were placed not for show, but for
reading. A massive low chest served as a coffee table
and Robin went closer to inspect the intricate carving.

"What an unusual piece," she commented, noticing
that the design was formed by strange birds and flowers
intertwined.

"Yes. I got it in Japan some time ago." He pressed a
panel on a side wall and a whole section slid noiselessly
aside, revealing a bar. "What would you like to drink?"

"Oh . . . um . . . I'll have whatever you're having."
That seemed safe enough, since she had no idea of the
correct thing to order after dinner.

He started to say something, thought better of it, and
poured two drinks into exquisite stemmed, cut-crystal
cordial glasses. The one he gave her had a dark brown
liquid in it, and as she reached for it their hands
touched and hers started to tremble. It was ridiculous
to be so nervous, she told herself. Hoping he hadn't
noticed, Robin held the delicate glass in both hands and
raised it to her lips.

"This is delicious," she pronounced. "What is it?"

"I thought you would like it—it's crème de cacao.
Like having a chocolate soda for dessert."

She looked at his glass and saw that it contained a
lighter liquid. "You're having something different."

He held his glass up and the light turned its contents
amber. "Yes, brandy. That's for big boys—chocolate is
for little girls."

Robin was furious. She was tired of being treated like
a child. How could she get him to take her seriously? "I
said I would have what you were drinking and I meant
it. This is delightful, but actually I prefer brandy."

"Oh, really? Then here—you can share mine." He offered her his glass.

Determinedly, she took a big gulp and thought for a minute that she had swallowed live coals! Her throat burned and tears came to her eyes. If I open my mouth I bet flames will come out, she thought, trying desperately not to cough.

Barely containing his amusement, he said, "My, you really are a big grown-up girl, aren't you?"

"What do I have to do to convince you?" she raged.

"There are ways." Carefully, he took the glass out of her hand and set it down with his on the chest. "Yes, there are ways," he repeated, slipping his arm around her waist.

Robin automatically stiffened but he held her close. His lips found hers in a kiss that was at first gentle and then increasingly insistent. His hands moved up and caressed her back, drawing her ever closer. Their bodies merged and she lost all will to resist. There was heaven in his arms, in his mouth, in his hard, lean body.

Finally, she forced herself to draw away, but where she found the strength, Robin never knew. They stood and looked at each other almost in awe.

Surprisingly, it was Calvin who broke the spell. Turning toward the stereo, he said, "I've been less than a perfect host. I forgot to put the music on. Let's see, isn't some romantic music like Montevani called for in a situation like this?" He smiled, his old suave self once more.

How does he do it, Robin wondered? How can he turn his emotions on and off like a thermostat? Her legs were trembling and her mouth tingled from his passionate kiss. Did it mean so little to him? That's the way men are and you shouldn't be surprised, she told herself. Especially this man. But it hurt all the same, and she was trying to think of a graceful way to say she wanted to go home when he beckoned to her. It was pride that forced her to join him as if nothing had happened. She would sooner die than let him know how he had stirred her emotions.

"Come see if there is anything you would rather hear."

She joined him and made a show of looking at the records. "I'm afraid I don't know very much about music," she managed in a small voice. "Art was more in my line."

"What kind of art do you like—old masters, modern—what?"

"A little of everything, really," she answered.

"You must have some favorites. Tell me." His amorous mood seemed to have dissipated and he was regarding her with interest instead.

"Well—" She thought for a minute. "I especially like Magritte. I tried to copy one of his paintings once. It looked so simple but it wasn't. Remember the huge rose that completely filled a room? He calls it *The Listening Chamber,* and until I tried to draw it I didn't understand why."

"Interesting that you should mention Magritte. Come with me." And he took her by the hand.

"Don't tell me you have an original!" she exclaimed eagerly. "The one I copied was out of an art book. I've only seen the real thing in museums."

He led her down a wide hallway to a large room at the end. Facing the door was not a circular, but a huge king-sized, bed, and Robin held back, realizing this was his bedroom.

"Don't let the bed throw you," he said. "It's

essential for sleeping. I tried the floor once and didn't like it."

She looked around the big room, fascinated in spite of herself. It was furnished as tastefully as the livng room and filled with objects from all over the world. A pair of beautiful silver and rosewood French dueling pistols were in a locked glass cabinet. On one wall hung a small Persian prayer rug alive with vibrant colors. Underneath was a brass table from India, supported by crossed ebony wood legs.

He watched her appraising the room and started to laugh. "In some respects you're no different from any other woman, are you?"

"What do you mean?"

"You're standing there thinking how you would redecorate."

"No such thing," she said. "I was just admiring your lovely things."

"Do you mean to tell me that, at the very least, you don't want to put a ruffled chintz cloth on that round table by the window?"

"Well . . . now that you mention it," she drawled, and they both laughed.

"Not until after we're married, and I doubt if even then," he told her firmly.

"No, I can see you're not the ruffly type," Robin agreed, thinking with a pang how easily he could joke about marriage. How many girls had been fed that line? And how many poor souls believed it?

"But that wasn't the purpose of this visit. I'm probably the only man who really meant it when he brought a girl to his bedroom to see—if not his etchings, then his oils." And he pointed behind her.

Turning around, Robin saw the Magritte on a wall by

the door. All of the artist's works were masterpieces but this was not one she would have chosen for herself. It showed a wispy lady's nightgown hanging from a wooden hanger, and protruding from the sheer material were two generous-sized breasts, the nipples rosy and erect. Wouldn't you know it, she thought—my favorite is a giant rose and his is—this. Drawing closer, she read the name plate underneath. It said, *"Philosophy in the Boudoir."*

"How do you like it?" he asked, watching her intently.

"It's very nice," she answered primly.

He ran his fingers through his hair in exasperation. "Robin, this time I really am annoyed with you. You profess to like art, yet you let yourself be put off by the sight of a woman's breasts. Don't you know that's one of the truly beautiful things in this world?"

Robin flushed painfully. "It's not that I don't like it. It just wouldn't be my first choice, that's all."

"What would be, some sweet little pastel of birds and butterflies?" he asked scornfully.

"I didn't say that."

"No, but you meant it. You're as bad as the mid-Victorians, do you know that? They used to call them limbs—when they mentioned them at all. But they're not limbs, they're arms and legs and hips and thighs. You probably can't even say the words. Why don't you see that your body is beautiful and was meant to give you pleasure? Life isn't a fairy tale. You're trying to make up your own rules and it won't work."

He stood over her and put his hands on her shoulders. "Is this all right?" Then he slid his hands down till they gently cupped her breasts. "But this wrong?"

She pushed violently against his chest but he imprisoned both of her hands in one of his and circled her slender waist with an arm of steel, holding her fast.

"No, I won't let you get away this time. I'm going to make you admit you're a woman, if it's only to yourself."

She struggled in a wordless panic but it was no use. He was too strong for her.

"What do you feel when I kiss you here?" he demanded, as his mouth sought the soft cleavage between her gently swelling breasts. "Or here?" And he kissed the hollow in her throat where a pulse beat wildly.

Suddenly he picked her up and carried her over to the bed, pinning her down so that all she could do was look at him with frightened eyes. Like a small quivering bird, she awaited the inevitable—all escape cut off. The soft bed enveloped her as she shrank away from the exultation in his blazing eyes. For a long moment he just stared at her and then the passion drained from his face. Relaxing his grip, he said, "You don't know what I'm talking about, do you? Come on—I'll take you home. Get your things."

The sudden change in him was so unexpected that for a moment after he released her Robin could only stare at him in bewilderment. What did it all mean? She sat up slowly, not knowing what to expect next. Was it some kind of trick?

But he turned away, and when he spoke his voice was cold and distant. "I said get your things."

She started to tremble as reaction set in and her eyes filled with tears. Would she ever know what this terrible man wanted from her? His passion was frightening enough, but the cold contempt in his voice was more than she could bear. It was a nightmare and she must get away from him—now, this very minute!

Taking advantage of the fact that his back was turned, she darted to her feet and ran wordlessly from the room, grabbing her things along the way. Dashing down the hall, she made straight for the front door and struggled with the massive latch, panicky for fear the door was locked. It only took a moment to discover it wasn't, but her heart was beating like a tom-tom and she was too upset to realize he wasn't following her.

Slipping out the door, she ran like a deer down the long driveway and over to the Dahlgren house next door. It was in merciful darkness and she crept noiselessly up to her room. Only after she had closed the door and leaned against it, panting for breath—only then did she feel safe. But now the tears came in earnest as she relived the awful scene in Calvin's bedroom.

Calvin's blazing eyes were burned forever in her memory. No man had ever looked at her like that before. She should have known better than to go to his house alone with him, but that was still no excuse. How dare he touch her like that and then be furious when she didn't respond like some . . . some . . . Robin hid her burning face in her hands, ashamed not only of his actions, but also her own. The truth she had been trying to conceal refused to stay hidden. Even in the midst of her terror, she had been thrilled by his warm lips on her bare skin.

What strange power did he have over her that could make her stray so far from her upbringing? She couldn't forget the lovely weak feeling that almost made her willing to give whatever he wanted. This was what the Sisters had warned her about.

Robin gave a little laugh that turned into a sob. He thought she didn't know what it meant to feel like a woman. Well, he was partially right—maybe she had never known before, but she knew now.

And what good did it do, this awakening? Calvin hated her. He thought she was cold, a lifeless doll instead of the passionate woman he wanted. It shouldn't matter what he thought. She ought to be furious with him, but even after all the indignities he subjected her to, there was this aching in her heart that only he could fill.

It was all over, of course, whatever there had been between them. But how could she ever face him again—not only tomorrow, but all the remaining days until she could go back to the blessed simplicity of life in San Francisco. At least, don't ever let me be alone with him again, she begged whatever Fates watch over star-crossed lovers.

Eventually she undressed and got ready for bed, praying for the oblivion of sleep. But it was a long time before her eyelashes finally drooped like fallen feathers on her pale cheeks.

Chapter Six

The next morning Robin woke late and with a raging headache. I should have been up hours ago, she thought, shocked when she looked at the clock. I wonder who got up with Dicky? It crossed her mind that for the first time she had shirked her duties and Mrs. Dahlgren was apt to be angry with her, but the thought brought no terror. The worst she can do is send me back to the mainland, Robin thought with something like relief.

But it wasn't her nature to avoid responsibilities, so she dressed swiftly and ran down the stairs, dreading the questions her lateness would provoke. She was certain that Pauline would want to know all the details of her date—who did you go with? where did you go? did you have a good time? Pauline was genuinely interested in Robin and from the first had tried to bring her into the fold. Now, after her first real date, there would be no avoiding the questions.

When she arrived in the dining room, however, she found she had been given a reprieve. There was news of much more importance and Pauline and her mother were discussing it avidly.

"Robin, I thought you'd never get up. Just wait until you hear! We've all been invited to the opening of Calvin's new hotel on Kauai. I didn't even know he had one—he never talks about himself. But evidently it's really elegant. We're going to stay overnight and be given the V.I.P. treatment and everything. How about that!"

"He's such a dear, thoughtful man. I always say that breeding shows." Mrs. Dahlgren beamed.

"Money doesn't hurt either," Pauline added, grinning.

Her mother frowned. "Don't be crass, young lady."

Undaunted, Pauline proceeded to fill Robin in on the details. "We're flying over late this afternoon. It's only about twenty minutes by plane. The opening is tonight and it's really going to be a blast! The television stations will be there and loads of celebrities. I bet they'll have gardenias floating in the pool and Mai Tais with orchids on top—the whole ball of wax."

"I wonder if my black chiffon would be appropriate," Mrs. Dahlgren murmured.

Robin swallowed and asked, "Is Dicky invited?" dreading the answer.

"Oh, no, it's quite inappropriate for a child," his mother said. "Calvin very kindly invited the whole family, but I've made arrangements for Dicky to stay overnight with the Engels. They're the friends we visited and he had a marvelous time with their children. He will be much better off there."

"Isn't it great, Robin. You won't have to be chasing after the little demon. We'll have a ball."

"It sounds lovely but I'm sure I'm not included in the invitation," Robin said.

"Of course you are. He said the whole family and you're family," her friend said positively. She looked at her mother and grinned. "I know why he wants Robin and me, but you and Dad probably were invited because he knew you wouldn't let us go without you."

"Perhaps he had another reason for wanting to get to know your parents," Mrs. Dahlgren said archly.

But Pauline was too excited to get embroiled in the same old argument and merely said, "Please don't start on that again."

It's probably true, though, Robin thought. When a man started courting not only the girl but her whole family, it was a sure sign. For whatever reason, Pauline wasn't ready to admit it, but her mother knew.

"We don't have much time and we have all kinds of decisions to make," Pauline said. "Darn that Calvin—he could have given us a little advance notice. But he probably wanted it to be a surprise. Come on—let's go look through the closet."

Robin felt it was time to put a stop to this once and for all, so she said, with all the firmness she could muster, "I'm not going. There is no reason for him to invite me and if he actually did, then he was just being polite. You go ahead and you can tell me about it when you get back."

"You're being downright tiresome," Pauline complained. "What do you want—a hand-engraved invitation? I'm going to call him right now and have him set you straight."

"No, don't do that," Robin cried in a panic.

"Yes, that's exactly what I'm going to do since you're being so stubborn."

As Pauline left the room, Robin jumped up, intending to stop her forcibly if necessary, but Mrs. Dahlgren intervened. "Would you please go out and check on Dicky?"

"Now?" Robin asked despairingly.

The older woman looked at her in surprise. "Yes, of course now. I told him not to go any farther than the patio, but you know how he gets carried away."

Robin glanced hopelessly toward the hall, but she couldn't ignore explicit instructions, so she did as she was told. He was playing happily with a sand pail and shovel, and after assuring him that she would return shortly, Robin went back in the house.

Pauline was just coming back into the room. "I hope you're convinced," she said with satisfaction. "I just talked to Cal and he said of course you must come. He said the only things you regret in life are the things you *don't* do and I was to tell you that specifically. He's right, too, you know."

Robin paled as she realized what he meant. Did Pauline suspect anything from his reckless message? She searched her friend's face, but it was filled only with happy anticipation.

There didn't seem to be any way to get out of going without making a big to-do, which would surely raise suspicions. Did he always get his own way? Robin wondered helplessly. With great reluctance she followed Pauline up to her room and together they

decided what they were going to take. Since this
occasioned many momentous decisions as well as a lot
of packing and unpacking, the afternoon flew by. When
it was time to leave they still weren't quite ready and
the Dahlgrens were waiting impatiently. At least, Mrs.
Dahlgren was.

"Girls, we're going to be late if you don't hurry," she
complained. "I don't know how it can take so long for a
simple overnight trip."

In spite of her fears, they arrived breathless but on
time at the airport and in due course boarded the
inter-island plane. It looked almost like a toy after the
giant jet liners but it was more fun in its way. Instead of
soaring up to an altitude of who knew how many
thousand feet, these small planes seemed to skim over
the treetops, affording a good look at the ground
below.

By this time Robin had seen a good bit of Honolulu,
but she had never been to the outer islands and it was
an interesting experience. First, they flew over a bright
blue ocean dotted with little white sailboats. Farther
out, two huge freighters were making for port, their
wake creating a widening V astern. And when they
reached Kauai she had a stunning view of the lush
tropical rain forests with towering trees that looked
from this altitude as though you could reach out and
touch the tips.

The plane put down all too soon on the landing strip
where cars and taxis were drawn up to meet the arriving
passengers. This quiet island had never experienced
such an influx and it was all due to Calvin. From chatter
overhead, it seemed that every incoming plane was
filled with people going to the Aloha Haole—his hotel.

It was going to be quite an event and the guests were already in a festive mood.

The only unwilling participant besides Robin was Mr. Dahlgren. Parties were not his thing and he had only come to this one because it was easier than facing the recriminations if he stayed home. An easygoing man, he could occasionally be pushed to the limit, and that was in danger of occurring any minute.

"How long do we have to stand around here?" he grumbled.

"Be patient, John, and do remember you're a guest," his wife reminded him. "It was marvelous of Calvin to invite us and the least you can do is stop complaining."

As though hearing his name mentioned, which would have been impossible in such a crush, Calvin materialized at her elbow. "Is everything all right?" he asked.

"It's positively thrilling," Mrs. Dahlgren twittered. "I do love openings—they're so glamorous. Isn't that the host of the morning TV show?"

He glanced over his shoulder and said, "Yes, you'll meet him tonight, but right now I imagine you would like to get settled in the hotel."

Mr. Dahlgren sighed with relief. "I always knew there was something about you I liked, my boy."

"I'm afraid the mob scene gets even worse"—Calvin grinned—"but at least you'll find your suite comfortable, I think."

As he shepherded the little party toward a waiting limousine, Pauline took his arm and started talking to him in a low voice. He bent his head attentively toward hers and Robin was left to bring up an uncertain rear. Calvin had ignored her so completely that she was left wondering if perhaps she was supposed to take the airport bus.

The chauffeur helped Mr. and Mrs. Dahlgren into the backseat and Pauline hopped in after them, saying, "Hey, don't forget Robin."

Calvin turned so abruptly that he bumped into her. Grabbing her elbows to steady her, he said, too softly for those in the car to hear, "Ah, yes, we mustn't forget the ice maiden. If you stay out in this hot sun too long you may melt, and then what would happen?"

Jerking her arms away angrily, she got into the limo and pulled down one of the jump seats, not waiting for any assistance. As the car pulled away, she turned her head and looked resolutely out the other window, blotting out his mocking smile.

It was only a short drive to the hotel and, since they were guests of the management, their path was smoothed at every turn. The bellman showed them directly to their suite, and when he opened the door Mrs. Dahlgren gave a small yip of pure pleasure. Accustomed as she was to luxury, this was the ultimate.

Two spacious bedrooms were on opposite sides of a huge living room that looked as though it belonged in Buckingham Palace. Besides exquisite furnishings and bouquets of fresh flowers throughout, every human desire seemed to have been anticipated and catered to. A low coffee table held a large basket of fruit, a box of candy, and a dish of nuts. On the long bar that filled half of one wall, a bottle of champagne was chilling in a silver cooler and a bottle of Scotch stood next to a filled ice bucket.

"Now there's a man who knows how to treat a guest," Mr. Dahlgren said, approaching the bottle of Scotch with enthusiasm.

"John, you're not going to have a drink now, are you?" his wife asked disapprovingly.

"Yes, I am, my dear—it has to be five o'clock somewhere."

"Isn't this place positively smashing?" Pauline asked, whirling around to take it all in. "I can hardly wait to see the rest of the hotel. Let's get dressed and go exploring."

The two girls went into the bedroom they shared and promptly popped out again to tell Pauline's parents about the splendors within. Then they had to inspect the other bedroom. All in all, it was later than planned when they finally got ready.

The sun had set and tiny stars were just starting to blink on. Music was coming from a large room and beautifully dressed people were streaming toward it. Most of the men wore white dinner jackets, for this was the tropics, but there was an occasional man in a plum-colored damask jacket or a powder blue brocade with satin lapels.

"Some of those men look fancier than I do," Robin said, giggling.

"Not so—you look super," Pauline assured her, and it was true.

Pauline had insisted that Robin borrow a dress for the occasion and the one they jointly chose was a flame-colored chiffon with an uneven petal hem that displayed her slim legs. The halter neck plunged to the waist, front and back, and the only decoration was a large flower of the same color and fabric at the very bottom of the deep-cut neckline.

"Sweet Charity!" Robin whistled when she first tried it on. "If the Sisters could see me now."

"You look fantastic," Pauline assured her. "Just be

careful when you bend over. It's all a matter of tension."

"You better believe I'd be tense if I ever appeared in public in this dress," Robin told her, but she allowed herself to be persuaded. Even she had to admit that the color did sensational things for her.

Pauline wore a long white silk gown that was draped Grecian-style from one shoulder and the two girls made charming foils for each other. As they walked in together, more than one head turned.

There was a dance floor in the middle of the large room, with tables all around it. As they hesitated in the doorway, the head waiter came up and, when Pauline gave her name, escorted them to a table right in front of the dance floor and facing the bandstand, where the entertainment would be.

"Now this is what I call first class," Pauline said with satisfaction. "This is the best table in the house."

Mr. and Mrs. Dahlgren arrived a few minutes later and took their places, but there were still many empty chairs. I wonder if this is Calvin's table, Robin questioned. Oh, no, it wouldn't be fair to have to spend a whole evening dodging his veiled barbs, unable to strike back without letting everyone know why. But apparently that was just what was in store for her because there he was!

Looking impossibly sophisticated and handsome in his dinner clothes, Calvin had joined them and was making introductions. A number of people trailed in his wake—some business associates with famous names, some celebrities. He introduced them to a flattered Mrs. Dahlgren, an unimpressed Mr. Dahlgren, and the two girls. Then, after seating them, he was gone again and didn't reappear until a fanfare announced that the show was starting.

Meanwhile, a whole bevy of waiters attended their table. Drinks appeared and turned out to be Mai Tais, just as Pauline had predicted.

"Watch out for those things—they're lethal," she warned.

Robin took a sip and licked her lips. "It's delicious—it tastes just like fruit juice."

"Famous last words!" Pauline took the glass from her hand. "Do me a favor. Wear the orchid in your hair, eat the fruit—do everything but drink it."

The man on Robin's right concurred. "I could tell you stories about Mai Tais that would trouble your dreams." And he proceeded to tell them a very funny one.

If it hadn't been for Calvin, Robin would have enjoyed the evening, but there was always the shadow of his presence. However, when he finally joined the table, he didn't speak to her and barely even glanced in her direction, which should have relieved her mind but in some perverse way didn't. She kept waiting for the boom to fall. It was psychological warfare at its worst. Occasionally she looked up and surprised his eyes on her, but they held an expression that defied definition.

The food was marvelous and the show was excellent. Her dinner companions were stimulating and the evening should have been perfect. Except for Calvin.

After the show, there was dancing. Calvin dutifully asked Mrs. Dahlgren to dance, thereby racking up more points with Mr. Dahlgren, who promptly got into a discussion with one of the attorneys who looked after the Carrington international interests.

Pauline and Robin were both asked to dance, but when she noticed that Calvin was politely working his way through all the ladies at their table, Robin's heart sank. How could she stand having his arms around her, trying to make polite conversation? He would undoubtedly save her till last because she was just an unpleasant duty he had to perform, but that was cold comfort. Maybe she could decline tactfully. Would he allow her that graceful exit or would he say something cruel and mocking, embarrassing her in front of all the others? The thought of it upset her so much that she missed a step and murmured an excuse to her partner.

By this time he had gotten around to Pauline, and as Robin watched them on the dance floor she felt a stab of misery. They looked so right together, both so handsome and assured. She was telling him something, and the look on his face as he listened twisted Robin's heart. It was so warm and tender, so amused in a fond, conspiratorial way. That's the way love should be, she thought—sharing and caring, not this constant turmoil I feel.

The number ended, and when her partner escorted her back to the table, the inevitable happened. Calvin and Pauline had also returned and Pauline said to her, "It's your turn now, Robin, and you're in for a treat. Cal is a divine dancer."

His arm was still around Pauline's waist and he squeezed her playfully. "Flattery will get you everywhere and I'm afraid you know it. You're a manipulative little minx."

They laughed together, obviously at some private joke, making Robin feel like an outsider. "Why don't you two dance another one?" she said. "I'd really rather sit down for a while."

"Nonsense, Cal is an experience no girl should miss," Pauline assured her.

"That's the consensus of opinion," he agreed, taking Robin's unwilling hand and leading her onto the dance floor.

The orchestra was playing a slow number and he tried to draw her close, but she tensed up instinctively, dreading the touch of his body against hers. Even with this small distance between them she could feel the animal magnetism radiating from him and smell the masculine scent of his after-shave lotion.

After trying unsuccessfully to steer her around the crowded floor, he said, "I know you can dance—I saw you doing it with Herb before." She tripped over his foot just then and turned crimson with shame. "But you're making things awfully difficult. I think it might be easier to push a department store dummy about."

"I'm sorry," she muttered, "I don't seem to be able to do anything to please you."

He raised one eyebrow sardonically. "Let's don't have any self-pity, my dear."

She raised her eyes furiously to his and said, "I'm not sorry for myself—I'm sorry for you because you think every girl you meet is going to drop into your hands like a ripe plum."

"I wouldn't say you were exactly a plum—more like a persimmon. And one that's not quite ripe at that."

"If you feel that way, there's no point in keeping up this stupid pretense. You've paid your duty dance." She tried to pull away, but he jerked her roughly against him, holding her so close she could hardly breathe. "You're hurting me," she protested.

Instead of loosening his grip, he tightened it. "Unless

you want to make a scene on the dance floor, you'd better relax and look like you're enjoying yourself."

"I could never enjoy myself with you," she said through clenched teeth.

"I think you could," he replied confidently. "Don't knock it till you've tried it."

"Oh!" her breath came out in a little gasp. "You twist everything I say around. You have an evil mind and you're a terrible man."

"That's the way you feel about sex, isn't it—that it's evil and terrible?"

"I didn't say that," Robin cried.

"But it's the way you feel—admit it."

How could they be having this conversation? It was worse than all the things she had dreaded when she knew she couldn't get out of dancing with him. "The difference between us is that all you think about is sex and that has nothing to do with love."

"You poor baby." He looked at her pityingly. "I see your education is sadly lacking in certain areas. I must say I feel sorry for the poor guy who gets you. He's going to have to be very patient."

"One thing you can count on—the man I marry isn't going to be anything like you," she said hotly.

There was mock horror in his face. "Don't tell me you intend to pick someone as inexperienced as you are? Good Lord, I can imagine your wedding night!"

A woman dancing by put her hand on Calvin's arm and Robin fervently hoped she hadn't heard his last words. "Marvelous party, darling—so glad you asked us," she trilled.

Calvin took her hand and kissed it, saying, "How could we have had it without you, Angela?"

Robin narrowed her eyes. "It's amazing how easily you can turn the charm on and off."

"You ought to try it sometime—it might help you get a husband," he told her. "That sharp tongue of yours never will, that's for sure."

"What business is it of yours?" she shot back, secretly hurt.

His eyes were brimming with deviltry. "I've always been interested in lost causes and it's my mission in life to see you married."

Fortunately, the music ended, and she wrenched herself from his embrace and headed back to the table, leaving him to saunter after.

"Wasn't I right—isn't he a dream to dance with?" Pauline was waiting for them.

"That doesn't begin to describe it," Robin said, and Calvin saluted her sardonically.

Pauline didn't notice, though, because her mind was on more urgent matters. "Robin, will you go to the powder room with me? I think this dress is hanging by a thread, and if I don't get some help immediately, I'm afraid I'll turn into one of those topless dancers."

They hurried off, Pauline clutching her shoulder, and, fortunately, the maid in the powder room was able to make emergency repairs.

As they were sitting side by side in front of the long mirrored dressing table, Pauline said, "Isn't that Calvin a dear?" and, not waiting for an answer: "Besides being kind and generous, he's a good friend. I don't think I've ever met anyone like him." She went on and on about him while Robin made needless repairs to her makeup. There didn't seem to be any obligation to reply and, besides, what could she say? Finally, Pauline seemed to sense a withdrawal on the other girl's part, and she said, "You do like him, don't you?"

Robin concentrated on a tiny speck of imaginary soot. "As you say, who wouldn't?"

Her friend looked at her with speculation. "Why do I get the feeling you said that with something less than enthusiasm?"

"I'm sure he's very nice. He isn't my type, that's all," Robin lied. "Too conceited for one thing."

"Conceited? Calvin? You must be joking! He's the most unaffected man I've ever known. He's one of nature's few noblemen."

The door of the powder room opened, sparing Robin the need to reply. It was one of the women from their table and they smiled at each other. "Lovely party, isn't it?" she commented.

"The greatest," Pauline agreed.

"You're from San Francisco, aren't you?" the woman asked.

"That's right."

"I thought I recognized you. I'm on the symphony board and you modeled for our spring benefit fashion show. I'm Mrs. Brittingham, by the way."

"Of course," Pauline beamed, "I remember now. It was great fun and I hope you'll ask me again."

"You don't know what you're getting yourself into, my dear," Mrs. Brittingham laughed. "We always need volunteers. This year we're having a dinner dance in the museum and we can use all the help we can get."

"That sounds lovely—what is the date?" Pauline asked.

Robin sat back, feeling very small. What was she doing in this company? These people were so polished and assured. They did the things she only read about in the newspaper. While they were going to charity balls, she had been caring for the little children in the orphanage. No wonder she didn't know how to act and Calvin found her so amusing. He could have been nicer about it, though. Pauline and the others didn't try to make her feel gauche as he invariably did. A small flame of anger started to kindle. If only there was some way to get back at him. Slowly, an idea began to form at the back of her mind. He was always ridiculing her for being Miss Prim and Proper. Suppose she turned the tables on him? What if she suddenly threw herself at him—up to a point, of course. Then, when he thought he'd made another conquest, she would say something like, "I really don't want to go on with this any longer. Suddenly, I find you terribly boring, darling." Could she deliver a speech like that convincingly?

Robin shivered with delight mixed with terror. For once she would have the upper hand, but Calvin would be absolutely furious! The thought gave her pause. She had witnessed the raw passion in this man, thinly veiled under a veneer of civilization. Was she playing with fire? But Robin refused to give up the idea. It was too soothing to all the wounds he had inflicted.

The other two had finished their chat and Pauline rose, saying, "Well, I think I'll make it through the rest of the evening now. Are you ready?"

"You go ahead," Robin told her. "I'll be along in a minute." But instead of going back to rejoin the party, she walked through the lobby and pushed open one of the heavy glass doors. The gardens were beautiful in the moonlight and she wanted to be alone for a while to savor the audacious plan that had occurred to her. Even if she never had the courage to go through with it, it was exhilarating to think about.

As she walked through the garden, Robin could tell that a lot of thought had gone into the landscaping and it showed. Pebbled paths led through spacious grounds and at every turn there was a delightful surprise, such as a splashing fountain or a lovely piece of statuary. She was beckoned ever farther, wondering what was around the next curve. It wasn't till she realized that the music was becoming very faint that Robin decided she had better turn back.

The paths were deserted by now, so when a man's voice spoke from the darkness, her heart leaped into her throat. Trying to penetrate the gloom, all she could see was the glowing end of a cigarette. Someone was waiting under a tree.

"Wh-who's there?" she asked, pausing uncertainly.

Calvin stepped out on the path where she could recognize him, but the tree branches threw shadows across his face. "Running away again?" he asked.

"You startled me!"

"Answer my question." His tone was short and peremptory.

Her heart was still pounding, but she answered, "No, of course I'm not running away."

"Then what are you doing out here all alone?"

"I . . . I just came out for a breath of air."

Leaning back against the tree, he folded his arms and looked at her cynically, taking in the fragile chiffon gown that lightly covered her slim body. "I wasn't aware that you were dressed so warmly. I'll have to tell them to step up the air conditioning. We wouldn't want the little ice maiden to thaw, would we?"

The simmering flame of resentment burst into full blaze and Robin threw caution to the winds. I'll do it, she vowed! If it's the last thing I ever do, I'll wipe that sneering look off his face.

Deliberately, she moved very close and rested her hip against his, propping her elbow against the tree trunk. "I don't know why you persist in thinking I'm cold," she said in honeyed tones. "Maybe you just haven't used the right approach."

He straightened up, and although his face was in deep shadow, she knew he was looking at her closely. "What new game are we playing now?" he asked.

"Why, the game of love, naturally, darling. And it's not new—it's old as the hills. You told me so yourself," she drawled, running her fingers through his hair.

"You're a lousy actress and, besides that, the role doesn't suit you. What's behind all this? What do you want?"

"What a silly question. I want you, of course." She slid her hand insinuatingly inside his jacket and then around to the back of his neck.

"Robin, do you know what you're doing?" he demanded.

"Not as well as you do, but I'm willing to learn." She fluttered her eyelashes at him and wondered if there was enough light for him to notice.

He pulled her hand down roughly. "You're a little fool, do you know that? Have you ever thought what would happen if you tried this on the wrong man?"

"How do you know I haven't?" she asked with a little laugh.

Calvin's fingers bit into her shoulders and he shook her so hard the barrette in her hair loosened, allowing a shining curtain to sweep across her cheek. This isn't going right at all, Robin thought. He was still treating her like a child. But she wasn't beaten yet.

Putting her arms around his neck, she lifted her face and gazed up at him seductively.

"Robin, I swear to . . ." he began, but she wouldn't let him finish.

"Don't talk," she said, covering his mouth with hers.

At first there was no response. In fact, for a moment Robin thought he was going to pull away from her the way she had done to him. Then his arms slowly wrapped her close and his lips parted slightly, seeking hers with increasing urgency. Their bodies were fused almost as one, and through the sheer fabric of her gown she could feel his hard, muscular loins.

An electric current ran through Robin's brain and in some dim corner a warning sounded. Now! Now is the time to deliver the coup de grace! But her body was powerless to obey. His mouth slid down to the hollow of her throat while she clung to him weakly. Then his lips touched her neck and slid across to her shoulder, pushing aside the flimsy fabric until her skin gleamed bare in the moonlight.

His mouth returned to hers and he gently guided her down to the soft carpet of the lawn. Lying in his arms, she was completely suspended in time. A night bird trilled a few joyous notes nearby and the scent of frangipani was heavy in the air. Calvin's kisses became more urgent and his hands caressed the gentle curves of her body, softly stroking her hip. Robin was stirred in a way she had never thought possible—beyond thinking, beyond caring. Only his touch mattered, creating a fire in her veins. This was what he had been trying to tell her and now she understood.

With a little moan, she wrapped her arms around his neck and crushed her body against his. Even this wasn't close enough—she wanted to be virtually a part of him.

The flame ignited him as well and he was breathing hard as he pinned her to the ground.

"My love, my dearest love," she breathed softly, waiting . . . waiting . . . But even as she looked at him with complete surrender, a change came over his face. All the ardor disappeared and left an expression she couldn't understand.

He pushed her away and stood up abruptly, leaving her lying there like a toy flung down by a careless child. "Get up. You'll catch cold lying there." His tone was brusque.

She felt as though someone had doused her with a pail of water. Bewildered, she got slowly to her feet, and he didn't attempt to help her. It was almost as if he couldn't stand to touch her.

"That was a fool stunt you pulled. Do you know what I almost—" He stopped short and turned to light a cigarette, which trembled in his fingers.

She stared at him, not comprehending. "But I thought . . ." Her voice trailed off. How do you tell a man that you thought he wanted you the way you wanted him?

As though reading her thoughts, he said, "You thought I wanted you that way, didn't you? Well, I don't." His voice was harsh and suddenly comprehension flooded over Robin.

She had thrown herself at him, offered herself—and been turned down! The humiliation was almost more than she could bear. Her eyes were dark pools of misery as she backed away from him in a kind of horror.

He started toward her saying, "You little fool, don't you know what I want?"

Mercifully, a group of late revelers came down the path, laughing and joking and spilling over into the garden beds. Robin took advantage of the distraction and darted around them back toward the hotel. They greeted Calvin like a long-lost friend, and by the time he extricated himself, Robin was in the elevator on the way to the safety of her room.

Please don't let Pauline be there, she prayed. I can't face anyone tonight—especially not her! And for once, Robin was in luck. The door to the Dahlgrens' bedroom was closed and the room she shared with Pauline was empty. Her friend was still out partying. Robin undressed quickly and got into bed, grateful for the reprieve.

She tried not to think of that dreadful scene in the garden, but it came sweeping over her like Niagara Falls, drenching her in shame. He had only been chasing her for the exercise. He wasn't even interested in her—*that* way. It was all a game, but I didn't know the rules, she thought miserably. When she remembered lying in his arms and declaring her love, Robin could have died. You weren't supposed to take that sort of thing seriously. As soon as he realized she meant it, he was really scared off. Maybe he even believed her when she pretended there had been other men and he didn't want to get involved with "used merchandise." Robin buried her face in the pillow, but the images wouldn't stop coming.

When Pauline came in much later, Robin lay very still, pretending to be asleep. It was only after Pauline got into bed and Robin heard her even breathing that she dared to move her position. Lying on her back, she stared at the ceiling. Tiny fingers of light were poking at the edges of the closed drapes before she finally closed her eyes.

Chapter Seven

Robin greeted the new day with a sinking dread, but it wasn't as bad as she had feared, except for having to listen to Pauline and her mother rehashing the party.

"Did you notice that dress she had on?" Mrs. Dahlgren asked, referring to a famous movie star. "I saw that dress at Maison d'Elle and I couldn't believe the price!"

"Everyone looked gorgeous, but more than that—I never met such fascinating people," Pauline said. "Isn't that Calvin something else? I don't think there is anyone he doesn't know. I was talking to one of his vice-presidents in this hotel thing and he told me they flew in a whole planeload of celebrities from the mainland."

"Was that the tall redhaired man you danced with so much?" her mother asked.

"Yes—he was great fun and a marvelous dancer."

"Well, I don't think you showed very good judgment," Mrs. Dahlgren said disapprovingly. "I hope you weren't doing anything as childish as trying to make Calvin jealous."

"Oh, Mother, for heaven's sake! Why would Calvin care who I danced with?"

"You know perfectly well why."

Pauline sighed. "What can I do to convince you that there's nothing between us? If I were in love with anyone you'd be the first to know it." But she seemed faintly uneasy and turned away so her mother couldn't examine her face. "Robin, what happened to you last night? You left while the party was still going on."

Robin gave full attention to plucking a dead leaf off the centerpiece. "I guess I'm just not used to such late hours."

"Well, you and Calvin are a couple of duds."

Robin looked up, startled. "Calvin?"

"Yes, he flaked out too. Say . . ." She looked appraisingly at Robin. "Is there anything going on that I should know about?"

Robin turned icy cold, but she managed to say, "Don't be silly. I told you he's not my type."

Fortunately, Pauline didn't pursue the subject.

After a leisurely lunch, they got their things together for the short trip home. The limousine was waiting for them at the door and the scene was almost the same as at their arrival except that Calvin was nowhere in evidence.

Mrs. Dahlgren was very upset. "I thought surely we'd see him in the lobby. How can we leave without saying thank you. I knew I should have phoned his suite, but you talked me out of it," she fumed.

"Oh, Mother, don't worry about it—he will be back

in a couple of days. You can thank him then," Pauline said impatiently.

"But it's such bad manners—what will he think of us?" Mrs. Dahlgren was still fussing when her husband urged her into the car.

For her part, Robin was grateful that she didn't have to face him, but it wasn't until she was finally settled in the plane that she dared breathe a sigh of relief. Given her kind of luck lately, she wouldn't have been surprised to find him in the next seat!

On the surface, life at the Dahlgren house seemed to return to normal, but there was a strange undercurrent of tension. Dicky was perhaps the only member of the household unaffected by it. He returned from his overnight visit full of stories to tell and plans for the immediate future—the only kind he cared about. Robin tried to appear interested in his projects because she loved him like a little brother, but all the joy seemed to have gone out of life. There were shadows under her violet eyes and she was getting thinner.

Mrs. Dahlgren was restless and out of sorts. The party on Kauai had been the high point of the season so far, but now that it was over, there wasn't anything special to look forward to, and she was a woman who had to have constant social engagements.

But the strangest one was Pauline. She seemed nervous and tense, completely unlike her old carefree self, and she hung around the house all day, which was most unusual. Pauline had mentioned that Calvin needed to stay at the hotel for a couple of days to be sure everything was running smoothly, so that explained why she was home instead of at his place. But it didn't explain her fixation with the telephone. Every time it rang, which was often, she ran to answer it before anyone else could get there.

I suppose she's waiting for him to call, Robin thought, willing herself not to care. But when she overheard one of Pauline's conversations, it was hard to keep her resolutions from crumbling.

It was early afternoon and Robin had come into the house to get a toy that Dicky wanted. Her bare feet didn't make a sound on the polished floor and Pauline's voice was clearly audible on the hall phone.

"I know—I miss you too, darling, but two days isn't so long." A pause and then: "Yes, it seems that way to me too, but we'll just have to wait."

Robin stole quietly back outside, tears misting her eyes. Did Pauline know how lucky she was? Evidently she did, since she was utterly miserable without him. Robin was miserable also, but the difference was there was no time limit for her. Life stretched out bleak and empty.

It was Mrs. Dahlgren who finally shattered the doldrums. "I have a perfectly marvelous idea," she announced. "We have been accepting Calvin's hospitality all the time we've been here and he has barely been in our house, which is disgraceful. So I've decided to give a party in his honor." She looked around brightly, expecting instant approval, but her husband was less than charmed at the prospect.

"Oh, good Lord," Mr. Dahlgren muttered. "I knew this peace and quiet was too good to last."

"Don't be so grumpy, John. "You know you like Calvin."

"Of course I like him—he's a splendid chap. Invite him to dinner anytime and I'll be delighted, but why does it always have to be a party? You just went to one—isn't that enough?"

His wife didn't even deign to answer such a foolish question, and, turning to the girls, she said, "I've been thinking about it and I've decided to have a real Hawaiian luau with poi and a whole pig roasted in a pit—everything."

Pauline made a face. "Have you ever tasted poi? It tastes like library paste."

"You don't have to eat it, but it's essential for authenticity. And I think I'll hire some native girls to serve and have them wear those sarong-type things."

"Mother, those 'native girls,' as you so naively put it, are American citizens and most of them are in college studying microbiology or some such."

"Well, you know what I mean. Honestly, Pauline, you're as bad as your father." Turning to Robin for support, she said, "Doesn't it sound like an exciting party?"

Robin was torn between her true feelings and sympathy for Mrs. Dahlgren. Her good nature won out and she said, "I'm sure it will be lovely."

"There, you see! At least Robin isn't a wet blanket like the rest of you."

Mrs. Dahlgren's enthusiasm was infectious, or maybe they all welcomed a diversion from their separate problems. For whatever reason, the house soon buzzed with activity and they were all caught up in it. There were a million details to be attended to—torches to light the patio, orchid leis for the guests, a Hawaiian steel band to play for dancing. Everything had to be tracked down and ordered. The phone rang constantly and Mrs. Dahlgren was never without a whole sheaf of lists. Everyone was pressed into service and Robin was kept too busy to think of anything except the party, which suited her fine.

In the midst of all the activity, Calvin returned home. The phone rang in the early afternoon and Pauline ran to it as usual, but this time Robin knew from her whoop of joy that it was finally the call she had been waiting for.

"Calvin, you darling, I thought you'd never get back." A pause and then a little laugh, "Of course that's the reason, but I missed you too."

It was a short phone call, and afterward Pauline started dialing furiously, calling the troops to action. Her face was lit with happiness when she came into Robin's room.

"Hey, guess what? Cal's back and we're all going over there for a swim. Finish up whatever you're doing and get into your suit."

"I couldn't possibly." Robin shook her head. "I have a million things to do for your mother."

"I'm sure they can wait. Come on. All the crowd will be there—Sally and Tom and Michael and . . .'"

"Michael?" Robin interrupted. "Michael Browning? I would have thought he'd left long ago. Surely the ship isn't still in port, is it?"

But Pauline was in a hurry to get ready and shrugged off the question. "I don't know—I suppose it must be."

She was gone in a rosy cloud of happiness, leaving Robin faintly puzzled. Wasn't the ship supposed to continue on after a short stay in Honolulu? Oh, well, what difference did it make?

Robin worked like a buzz saw all day. She was too busy to join the revelry next door, but she couldn't stop Pauline from telling her about it. Pauline was a changed person since Calvin's return. She didn't jump every time the phone rang, which was natural, of course, and she wasn't as tense, although she did appear to be charged with a curious excitement. It was the next day that Pauline decided she had to have a new dress for the party.

"Not another new dress!" her mother exclaimed.

"This is a very special event, isn't it? You were complaining because I wasn't getting into the spirit of things. Well, now I am." She turned to Robin and asked, "What are you going to wear? Do you need something new too?"

Robin considered telling Pauline that she had no intention of attending the party, but she knew it would only lead to endless arguments or an explanation that she couldn't give. She had anticipated the problem and worked it all out in her mind. The night of the party she would get dressed and go down as expected. Then, when all the guests started arriving, it would be a simple matter to disappear into her room. Who would ever notice? In answer to Pauline's question she merely said, "No, I'm all set, thanks."

"Good, then you can give me your undivided attention and help me pick out something glorious. We'll go to the Ala Moana shopping center. I've been meaning to take you there anyway."

"You can't go this morning," her mother told her. "Your father took his car and went downtown and I need the other car for errands."

"Oh, blast it!" But Pauline was only momentarily inconvenienced. "I know! I'll ask Cal to drive us."

"Wait!" Robin half rose from her chair. "We could take the bus or something," she called plaintively, but Pauline was gone. The shopping center was a long distance from the house and she didn't think she could bear being cooped up in a car with the two of them. But fortune was definitely against her, because Pauline came back in just a few moments with a satisfied smile on her face.

"Get ready, Robin. Cal will pick us up in fifteen minutes."

"I really don't think I should go," Robin began desperately. "I have to keep an eye on Dicky. Your mother can't possibly watch him with all she has to do and I can't just desert her."

"No, it's all right, dear. Mrs. Ching has kindly promised to let Dicky help her make cookies, and that will keep him busy for hours," Mrs. Dahlgren said. "You two girls run along and have a good time."

That effectively cut off all routes of escape, so Robin went upstairs and ran a comb through her hair. She didn't bother to change clothes, though. What for?

Pauline called to her as a horn tooted outside and Robin went reluctantly down to the front hall. Now I know how Marie Antoinette felt, she thought. Calvin was waiting by the open door and Robin looked at the sleek little car with loathing, remembering the last time she had been in it and all the romantic fantasies she'd had then. She was very conscious of him standing beside it but couldn't bring herself to look at him.

"Good morning, Robin," he said pointedly.

She was forced to look at him then and found his dark eyes fixed intently on her. She managed to murmur a greeting, but her heart was pounding and she knew her pulse was racing. He was so handsome lounging there in a cream-colored silk shirt with an ascot tied carelessly at the throat. It was no wonder all the women were in love with him. She probably wasn't the only one to make a fool of herself over this man.

But that scene in the garden came back once more to haunt her and she almost turned and ran back in the house. Luckily, Pauline's voice brought her to her senses before she did something foolish.

"You get in the middle, Robin," she said. "You have on jeans and you can straddle that console thing. I guess I should have worn jeans instead of a skirt, but I thought this would be easier for trying on clothes." And then to Calvin: "Couldn't you have brought the bigger car so we wouldn't be squashed in?"

"You are a spoiled brat, do you know that? Here I drop everything to satisfy your slightest whim and then you complain about my car." But he was laughing.

When Calvin slid behind the wheel, Robin tried to make herself as small as possible, yet, in spite of her efforts, their bodies were in contact. She was painfully conscious of the pressure of his thigh against her leg. Their shoulders met and his arm brushed against her as he reached for the gear shift.

"Sorry," he murmured perfunctorily.

In an attempt to avoid touching him, she put both feet on the middle console, which raised her knees almost to her chin in an impossibly awkward position.

His fingers gripped her knee as he pushed her leg down none too gently. "Will you stop acting like a little idiot," he muttered between clenched teeth, too low for Pauline to overhear.

Pauline was too busy chattering on about the hotel opening to notice anyway. "We didn't get to talk much about it yesterday, Cal, but it was absolutely fabulous. I think we closed up the place. It was really late when I got back to the room. What happened to you and Robin—you missed half the fun."

"We had fun in our own way, didn't we, Robin?"

There was a wry twist to his mouth as he glanced briefly at her.

Turning toward him she said softly, "That was a rotten thing to say!"

He matched his tone to hers, "Would you rather I'd told her what we really were doing—or, should I say, almost did?"

Pauline reached over and turned down the radio, complaining, "I can't hear a word you two are saying."

"I don't know what Calvin did," Robin said, going back to Pauline's question. "I went to bed."

"Knowing you, I'm not surprised." Her friend sighed.

"Oh, I don't know—sometimes our little Robin is full of surprises," Calvin said, and all Robin could do was sit there and swallow the angry words that sprang to her tongue.

Oh, how she hated him! It was agony being this close, having to feel the weight of his body against hers. And as if that wasn't bad enough, every time he shifted gears his leg slid up and down her own. He was enjoying her misery so much that when they stopped at a traffic signal, he put his right arm along the back of the seat as though to stretch, and Robin was caught unwillingly in an embrace that looked so casual she couldn't complain. His sheer masculinity caused her heart to pound and Robin didn't know if she was angrier at him or at herself.

Pauline was serenely unconscious of the tension building in Robin. She was concentrating on the coming shopping spree and asked Calvin, "When are you coming back to pick us up? Not too soon—I have a million things to get."

He looked at his watch. "I was going to take you to

lunch, but since it's ten thirty already, I don't suppose that would give you enough time."

"No thanks—Robin and I will grab a quick sandwich somewhere. You can buy us a drink instead."

They discussed the time and place as Calvin pulled into the mall and Pauline hopped out of the car, anxious to get started. Robin disentangled her legs from his, wild with relief at finally getting away from him. Skirt or no skirt, she decided, Pauline was going to sit in the middle going home.

As she slid across the leather seat, he caught her wrist, halting her precipitous flight. Leaning so close his lips brushed her ear, he said, "Buy something special. If you look beautiful at the luau I might reconsider your offer."

Robin gasped! How dare he remind her of *that?* Giving him an outraged look, she slammed the car door so hard the windows rattled.

"Come on—we have some serious shopping to do," Pauline called.

Robin had never seen anything like the Ala Moana Shopping Mall and she was amazed at its size. There were several levels with escalators going up and down to stores of every description. "You could get lost in here and never find your way out," she marveled.

"Not really," Pauline laughed, "although people have lost their cars temporarily. One poor lady forgot what level she parked on and the police had to drive her around for hours until they found it."

"I'm not surprised."

"Let's look for dresses first," Pauline suggested. "Have you decided what you're going to wear?"

"I'm not . . ." Robin paused in midsentence. She

had been about to say, "I'm not going," but stopped just in time. Instead she changed it to, "I'm not sure yet."

"Maybe we'll find something you can't resist and then you'll change your mind about buying something new." Robin didn't bother to argue with her and Pauline continued, "I know exactly what I want. Or at least I know the color."

"Well, that's half the battle. What color are you looking for?"

"I want something really foxy in white. A regular knockout of a dress."

"Who are you planning to knock out?" Robin asked, and then could have kicked herself. What a stupid question! She knew perfectly well who Pauline planned to enslave.

Pauline paused indecisively. "Robin, I've been wanting to talk to you for days, but I wasn't sure if . . ."

For the first time, she seemed ill at ease and comprehension flooded over Robin. She wants to tell me she's come to an understanding with Calvin, but she doesn't know how I'll take it. With a sinking feeling, Robin thought, I must have given myself away somehow because she knows, or at least she guessed, how I feel. What can I say to convince her she's wrong? Oh, please let me think of the right words! Above all else, Pauline must never know.

Playing desperately for time, she turned toward a store window full of elegantly gowned mannequins and quickly said, "Oh, look, there's a white dress. Let's go in here." They entered the shop and the moment for confidences passed.

A saleslady approached and Pauline explained what

she wanted. In a short time the woman reappeared with her arms full of dresses, only one of which was the right color.

"I didn't have much in white but I brought some other things I thought you might be interested in," she said.

Robin eyed a long turquoise gown completely covered with paillettes. It was slit to above the knee and glistened in the light. "This would look absolutely gorgeous on you."

Pauline fingered the delicate fabric critically. "It's pretty but not what I had in mind. Why don't you try it on?"

Robin looked at the price tag and gulped. "It's not what I had in mind either."

The saleswoman was holding up a short gown whose black long-sleeved top had a low décolletage. The skirt was shocking pink organza, deeply draped like a full-blown rose.

Robin's eyes lit up when she looked at it. "I must be easy to please—I love every one of them," she said.

But Pauline didn't. "No, no, none of those will do," she said impatiently. "They're all the wrong color."

"You have that lovely dress you wore on Kauai. Why do you want another white dress?" Robin asked, mildly surprised that her friend was so adamant.

"White shows off my tan best. What's the point of spending all that time in the sun if nobody notices?"

The next store they tried had nothing that pleased her either, so they tried another and still another. Robin was dizzy from looking at gowns and Pauline was almost in tears, which was completely unlike her. The dress was assuming an importance out of all keeping with the event.

"What on earth am I going to do?" she wailed.

Robin patted her hand. "Don't worry. We'll shop till midnight if we have to, but we'll find it."

And finally their determination paid off.

"Oh, Robin, this is it. This is *it!*" Pauline was standing in the dressing room in front of a three-way mirror that gave back multiple images of her tall, slender figure garbed in a shimmering sheath. The gown was cut simply but completely covered in crystal bugle beads, and the effect was one of total elegance. A dress that cried out for a special occasion.

Her dark hair framed a face vibrant with happiness and a lump rose in Robin's throat. For the first time, Pauline looked positively beautiful, and she knew it was because of Calvin. If he weren't already in love with her, he would be when he saw her like this.

"It's exactly what I want. I'll take it," Pauline told the saleslady, and, throwing her arms impetuously around Robin, she exclaimed, "I've got to tell you something."

Breaking away, Robin said in a strangled voice, "In a minute—there's something I want to look at outside."

She almost ran out of the dressing room, straight through the shop to the outside. Taking deep breaths of fresh air, she leaned her forehead against the cool glass of the store window, fighting for control. I'm happy for her, I really am, Robin told herself. It's only that I can't bear to hear about it just yet.

By the time Pauline came out with a big box under her arm, Robin had composed herself. The other girl looked at her strangely, but Robin managed to say, "Does that take care of our shopping for today?"

Pauline consulted her watch. "No, we have time yet, and I want to get some lingerie." She mentioned a well-known specialty store. "Let's pop in there and see what they have."

Robin watched in amazement as Pauline went through shops and boutiques like a locust with a charge account, acquiring everything in her path. She bought satin nightgowns lavishly trimmed in lace, perfume, panty hose—whatever caught her eye.

"When the bills start coming in, your father is going to murder you," she suggested.

The other girl just laughed. "Not Dad—he's a pussycat. Besides, it's all in a good cause."

"What's the good cause?"

Pauline looked at her friend with narrowed eyes. She seemed to be considering something but evidently decided against it, because she merely said lightly, "Well, I'm his only daughter. When I point out how much worse it could be if there were several of us, he'll pay the bills out of sheer gratitude."

Robin just shook her head at this logic. They were both weighed down with packages, and eventually Pauline either ran out of things to buy or stopped from sheer exhaustion.

Juggling her bundles in an attempt to see her watch, she said, "We're kind of late. Cal will probably be wild. I don't know where we're going to put all these boxes in that little car of his."

"I didn't think of it before, but why didn't we have some of these things delivered?" Robin asked.

"Oh, we'll manage somehow," Pauline answered evasively, and Robin thought, I never realized it before, but she's just like Dicky. She wants everything right this instant.

When they got to the little cocktail lounge where they were to meet Calvin, they found him already waiting and none too patiently. Getting up from the leather booth, he said, "Where in blazes have you been? If I were your husband I'd put you over my knee!"

He'd better get used to it, Robin thought grimly. I would have been frantic if I'd been even a few minutes late, but she's going to lead him a merry chase and it serves him right.

Indeed, Pauline didn't seem a bit concerned about the time. She slid into the booth, saying, "Don't be such a bear or I won't tell you about all the smashing things I bought."

He looked at the assorted packages. "Don't tell me all these things are yours? Didn't you buy anything?" he asked Robin.

"I didn't have time. I was too busy helping Pauline boost the Hawaiian economy singlehandedly."

Calvin moved a box that was digging into his ribs. "Now there's a girl after my own heart." He looked Robin up and down. "I never knew a woman who could go shopping without buying something." Turning to Pauline, he shook his head. "And as for you, I sincerely hope you marry a rich man."

Their eyes met meaningfully and Pauline smiled at him, a singularly sweet and gentle smile. "You can both kid me all you like—I don't think anything would upset me today."

Robin dropped her eyes, feeling like an intruder. They were undoubtedly wishing they were alone. If she weren't here they would probably be holding hands, their heads close together so that he could tell her in a low voice how much he loved her. To her horror, Robin felt tears forming under her long eyelashes, and she thought, I can't cry here—that would be too awful!

Sliding out of the booth, she said, "I'll be right

back," and before Calvin could get to his feet, she hurried to the ladies' room.

Staring at her sad, pale face in the mirror, Robin couldn't help contrasting it with Pauline's radiant one. And why shouldn't her friend be happy? She had won the prize. Of course, there was never any contest. Pauline was the one he would hold in his arms. She would feel his lips, demanding, seeking . . . Robin closed her eyes to shut out the picture. This is madness and I truly am an idiot, like he said.

She ran cold water over her wrists and it had a calming effect. Rummaging in her purse, she found a lipstick and then a comb. It didn't matter what she looked like, but at least this would give them a few more minutes alone and lessen the time she would have to spend with them. At last there wasn't anything else left to do, so she pinched her cheeks to give them a little color and took a last look in the mirror. I really do look like a poor little orphan waif, she thought, and smiled in spite of herself as she pushed open the door.

The way back from the powder room led down an aisle lined with high-backed leather booths. She had to go the length of the aisle and then around the end booth and back to the one in the middle where Calvin and Pauline were sitting. The backs were too high to see over but she could hear the tinkle of ice and occasional snatches of conversation. It was while she was walking as slowly as possible that she heard their voices.

"Oh, Calvin, you've been so wonderful to me. I don't know what I'd do without you." Pauline's joyful tones were unmistakeable.

His voice was serious as he answered her. "I wish I

knew if we're really doing the right thing. Are you absolutely sure about this?"

It was almost like singing when she said, "Sure? I was never more so in my entire life."

"You've very young, my dear, and I worry about that."

"I'm not *that* young," she protested, "and I've gone out with loads of boys. But that's all they were—boys. I didn't even know it, but I was looking for a man and now I've found one."

Robin was rooted to the spot. She knew it was hateful to eavesdrop on their conversation but she was powerless to move.

"Well, if you're absolutely certain . . ." He seemed strangely reluctant. "The only thing I insist on is that you tell your father. Tonight, you understand?"

"I promise, and stop looking so worried. He's going to be delighted. You're a darling and I love you. In fact, to prove it I'm going to name our first two children Calvin."

"Two of them? Then I sincerely hope at least one is a boy."

Robin felt faintly ill as realization swept over her. They must actually have set the date—that's what Pauline had been trying to tell her. She had been torn between sharing her happiness and keeping it a secret until after she told her father, as Calvin insisted. No wonder she was shopping up such a storm, confident that her Dad wouldn't object since it was "in a good cause." Pauline had started buying her trousseau! It was all clear now—the luau was to be an engagement party.

People were walking toward her, brushing past in the

narrow space, and Robin knew she couldn't stand there forever. Somehow she forced herself to continue down the aisle. They were still laughing when she joined them at the table.

"We ordered you a drink," Pauline told her. "Sit down and taste it before it gets all watery."

Robin thanked her and slid onto the banquette, sipping her drink as she was told. She glanced up to find Calvin looking at her intently. "Are you all right?" he asked.

Did he know that she overheard their conversation? Robin wondered, ashamed at what she had done. And did he think it mattered to her one little bit? She certainly wasn't going to give him that satisfaction. Raising her chin and willing it not to quiver, she said coolly, "Of course—why wouldn't I be?"

He frowned at her and turned pointedly to Pauline, ignoring Robin as though she weren't even there.

They finished their drinks and then loaded Calvin down with most of the packages. All the way to the parking lot, Pauline kept up a constant chatter about perfectly trivial things. She was wound as tightly as a coiled spring, practically exploding with suppressed emotion. By contrast, Robin and Calvin were unusually quiet. Both were caught up in their private thoughts, but Pauline either ignored the fact or else didn't seem to notice.

When they reached the car, Robin stood aside for Pauline to get in first. In a very firm voice she said, "You get in the middle this time." And although she had anticipated an argument, Pauline got in without a murmur.

It was something of an anticlimax. Whenever you gear yourself for battle and then meet no resistance, you feel kind of foolish, Robin thought wryly. But it was obvious that Pauline really wanted to sit next to Calvin. She would undoubtedly welcome having her leg nestled against his all the way home.

After helping Robin into the car, Calvin put his finger under her chin and, tipping her face up, looked at her searchingly. "You don't look well. Are you sure you feel all right?"

She jerked her chin away and said, "I'm perfectly fine, thank you, but even if I weren't, you have nothing to worry about. I won't get close enough to breathe any germs on you."

He scowled and angry words sprang to his lips, but he checked them. Instead, he raised one eyebrow and looked at her insolently. "What makes you think you'll get the chance?" he drawled.

"Come on, you two, stop clowning around," Pauline said. "It's getting late."

Calvin immediately straightened up, and this time it was he who slammed the door so hard that the little car shook.

Chapter Eight

The day of the luau dawned bright and clear and everyone in the Dahlgren household breathed a sigh of relief. Although Hawaiian weather is generally glorious, an occasional storm can mar its perfection. On those rare days, the sky turns a mutinous gray and palm trees bow low to the ground as if to propitiate the angry gods. It is then the tourists begin looking up plane schedules, only to see the skies clear and the sun come out like a benediction.

The squalls never last long but even the threat of one would have been enough to induce hysterics in Mrs. Dahlgren. Preparations had been proceeding well all week, and on this final day the house was in a complete uproar. Everyone was up early because sleep was impossible.

Poor Mr. Dahlgren was utterly miserable. He seemed to be in the way no matter where he went and finally, in desperation, announced that he was leaving. While his wife was secretly happy to see him go, she felt, quite unreasonably, that he ought to show more enthusiasm for a party he didn't want in the first place.

"Be sure to come home early, John. I have enough on my mind without worrying about you being late."

"I wouldn't miss it for the world," he said, giving her a kiss on the cheek and winking at the girls.

"I want to go to the party too," Dicky said, banging his cup on the table. His lower lip stuck out ominously. The plans were for him to stay overnight at Mrs. Dahlgren's friends' and he was having none of it.

"Now don't start that again," his mother warned. "You know you have a wonderful time with Buddy and Caroline." Almost to herself, she remarked, "When this is all over we really must have them here to visit."

"I *don't* have a good time. I *hate* it there! I want to go to the party."

He looked on the verge of tears and Robin put her arm around him. "You don't want to go to any old grown-up party—they're no fun."

"Yes they are too."

"I'll tell you what—you don't have to leave till this afternoon, so suppose we go out after breakfast and watch them dig the hole."

The pièce de résistance of every luau is a whole pig wrapped in ti leaves and roasted in a huge pit dug right in the damp sand. Two men were already at work on it because the meat had to roast for about eight hours buried in live coals.

"I don't think that's such a good idea," Dicky's mother said. "I'm afraid he might fall in, and even if he doesn't, he's sure to get in their way. Why don't you take him over to Calvin's for a swim?"

"No!" Robin said sharply, and flushed self-consciously as Mrs. Dahlgren looked at her in surprise. "I mean . . . well, he might be busy, and we don't want to just barge in on him. Why don't I take Dicky for a long walk down the beach?"

"Well, if you think that would be better." Mrs. Dahlgren's attention had already wandered back to the long lists of things that still had to be checked off. As long as Dicky was taken care of and not underfoot, she was satisfied.

Robin and Dicky went out into the clear sunny morning and the little boy ran directly to the spot where two handsome Hawaiian youths were digging in the sand, their muscles rippling across suntanned backs. It was predictable and she couldn't really blame him. Even grown men sometimes stand for hours watching a sidewalk excavation. What could be more irresistible to a small boy?

A luau pit is much more than a big hole in the ground. It must be dug by experts according to an ancient art. Broad, flat stones are carefully placed to form a virtual underground oven, and unless properly constructed, the whole thing will collapse. These young men knew their craft and Robin was as fascinated as Dicky, but mindful of the fact that his mother didn't want him there, she finally managed to coax him away.

Dicky was by no means over his bad temper, however, and when they got to the water's edge he started to run away from her down the beach.

She ran after him, shouting, "Come back here, you little demon!" but he merely looked over his shoulder and laughed, running like the wind.

A man coming out of the surf just ahead saw what was happening and stretched his arms wide, intercepting the child as he tried to dodge past. Racing up to them, Robin saw that it was Calvin, but she was so grateful she didn't care. So much could happen to a little boy who got too close to that deceptively calm ocean.

Panting, she said, "Thank goodness you caught him! He's absolutely possessed by the devil today. I've never seen him this way."

Calvin slung Dicky under one arm, carrying him back from the water. "What's the matter, sport? Were you running away from home?"

"Yes. They're mean to me and I don't want to live there anymore." He looked up with an impish expression. "How about I come live with you?"

"Well, now, let's sit down and discuss it." He dumped the little boy unceremoniously on the sand and, picking up the towel he had left by his beach thongs, started to dry himself off.

Dicky knew that when adults "discussed" things the decision usually went against him so he stuck out his lower lip and stated, "I want to come live with *you.*"

"That might be a bit of a problem, champ. Who would look after you?"

Dicky considered this and came up with an immediate solution. "Robin could come too."

Calvin looked at her appraisingly and she had an almost uncontrollable urge to tug at her bathing suit to make sure it was in place. But she knew that would only produce an amused smile from this infuriating man. "Don't be ridiculous, Dicky," she said crossly.

"Let's not dismiss it too hastily. Maybe he has a good idea after all," Calvin said.

"Why are you encouraging the child?" Robin cried. "He thinks you're serious."

"How do you know I'm not?" When she stamped her foot in rage, Calvin turned to Dicky and shook his head. "I'm afraid it's no go. Robin doesn't want to come live with us."

"You can make her," Dicky said positively. He was so used to getting his own way that it didn't occur to him an adult could be thwarted.

"I don't know about that." Calvin was doubtful. "I don't think Robin even likes me."

"Yes she does. She talks about you all the time to Pauline."

Robin gasped. "That's not true and you know it!"

Dicky was supremely disinterested. "Anyway, you can make her do it. Just tell her she has to—that's what Mommy does."

Calvin was enjoying himself immensely. There was suppressed mirth in his voice as he said, "I don't think I could convince her, but I suppose I could do what the cavemen did."

"What did they do?" the little boy asked, immediately intrigued.

As much as she loved Dicky, Robin felt like strangling him at the moment, and Calvin too. The little boy had no idea what he had provoked but Calvin was going along with it just to humiliate her. As he got lazily to his feet, she faced him with angry words on her lips— words that were never uttered.

Moving with catlike speed, he put his hands on her waist and lifted her effortlessly into the air, slinging her over one shoulder and holding her there in a viselike grip. "See? This is the way cavemen subdued their quarrelsome women," he told the little boy, who was delighted by the feat.

Robin struggled to get down, but Calvin merely encircled her with both arms, holding her so tightly against him that all she could move were her arms and legs. She was terribly aware of their bodies touching and this time there wasn't even a scrap of sheer fabric covering his upper torso.

"Are you crazy?" she demanded.

"I'm just trying to give you what you think you want."

She hammered on his back with small clenched fists, furious at him for bringing up that awful time at the opening of his hotel and also for manhandling her in front of the child. "Put me down this minute," she demanded.

Dicky was enchanted and danced around them, clapping his hands. "Don't do it," he chortled, delighted with this new game he thought they were playing for his benefit.

It seemed like an eternity but it was probably only a moment until he lowered her gently to the ground. Her body slid sensuously along his and she was painfully conscious of his broad shoulders and chest, his slim waist and flat stomach. Until her feet touched the ground she had to hold on to him and she hated herself for not wanting to let go. No matter how much she loathed this man, every time he touched her, she couldn't help being deeply disturbed. And the worst part of it was he knew it!

He steadied her for a moment with one arm around her waist and the other on her shoulder. They looked at each other and his eyes had pinpoints of fire in them. Slowly his hand slid up from her shoulder, his thumb and forefinger moving gently up and down, massaging the soft skin at the nape of her neck. Her lips parted and she looked at him, wanting to break away yet completely defenseless.

Dicky's piping little voice brought her back to reality. "I want to go swim in the pool now."

Robin drew back from the brink of disaster, ashamed to let him see how shaken she was. He was a cruel and predatory man. Why couldn't he leave her alone? He didn't want her—he just liked to torment her, to reaffirm his power over all women. It didn't matter that he was in love with Pauline. This was just fun and games—an exercise for his masculine ego. But Robin felt deeply disloyal to her best friend, ashamed of how her pulses raced when he held her close. It must never happen again! He thought it was a lark to play on her emotions, but Robin made a solemn vow never to let him touch her again.

As if to make a mockery of her vow, he caught her by the elbows and pulled her around to face him. "You're embarrassed, aren't you? What does it take to make you admit you're human like the rest of us, with normal, honest feelings?"

"Let go of me!"

But he only held her tighter. "Not until you tell me you didn't enjoy being in my arms."

In desperation Robin wrenched herself from his grip and grabbed Dicky by the hand. "Come on—we're going home."

He hung back, saying, "No, I don't want to."

Although she didn't realize it, she gave him a little shake and said through clenched teeth, "I said we were going home *now!*"

Looking up at her in pure wonder, Dicky decided

that for once in his life he had better do as he was told. Trotting along beside her, his little legs struggling to keep up, they sped down the beach. He looked over his shoulder once, but Robin raced along as if pursued by devils.

The afternoon sped by in a flurry of activity. After Dicky was packed off to the Engles', Robin was needed to help Mrs. Dahlgren with the party. Round tables covered with colorful cloths were already set up on the patio, but the centerpieces and candles had to be arranged in the middle. The florist had delivered bowls of red and pink anthuriums, those waxy tropical blooms that are so perfect they actually look artificial, and Robin placed an arrangement in the center of each table. Then the tall, tapering candles had to be put in holders. She lettered place cards and put them out, saw that the candy dishes were filled, and attended to a million and one little details.

Her job was complicated by the fact that every few minutes Mrs. Dahlgren would call her off of one task and set her to doing another, but Robin didn't mind. She was happy to be kept busy and also realized that her employer was a bundle of nerves by this time.

"I do hope we've thought of everything," Mrs. Dahlgren said distractedly.

Robin tried to soothe her. "It all looks lovely. Why don't you go up now and take a little rest?"

"Oh, I couldn't possibly! I'm just sure I've forgotten something."

"I can't imagine what it could be."

"About the other flowers . . . I'll have them brought out to the front hall before the party begins, and when the guests arrive, a lei should be placed around each one's neck," Mrs. Dahlgren instructed. Robin had already peeked inside the huge florist boxes resting now in the refrigerator. Half of them contained delicate garlands of tiny vanda orchids in a lovely shade of lavender, looking like miniature ruffled angel faces. The other half were waxy white blossoms that looked like stars and smelled like heaven.

"It doesn't matter what is put on the men but a little judgment should be exercised with the women." At Robin's questioning look she said, "I mean, if she has on an orange dress, for heaven's sake she shouldn't be draped in orchids."

"And they're to be kissed on both cheeks," Pauline added, coming into the room. "Mother wants it to be absolutely authentic and that's an old Hawaiian custom. Also a good way to get acquainted fast." She grinned. "Oh, and Mother, I have one more for your guest list," Pauline said casually.

"Pauline, you didn't!" Mrs. Dahlgren was exasperated. "How could you invite someone at the last minute like this? The tables are all arranged and the place cards laid out. How could you do this to me?" Almost as an afterthought, she asked, "Who is it?"

"His name is Michael Browning."

Her mother knitted her brows in thought. "That name sounds familiar. Where do I know it from?"

"He was on the ship coming over with us."

"I don't remember—" A look of outrage crossed Mrs. Dahlgren's face, and she asked, "Was he that young officer who monopolized all your time?"

"He didn't exactly force his attentions on me, Mother, but yes—that's the one."

"What on earth did you invite him for and what is he

still doing here anyway? Didn't that ship leave ages ago?"

"I believe he left the ship. I don't think he works for them anymore."

"All the more reason not to invite him. What is your connection with this young man?" Mrs. Dahlgren was working herself up into a real fit of temper, remembering the arguments she had had with her daughter on the cruise.

"He's a friend of Calvin's. I've seen him over there at swimming parties." Pauline looked at her mother evenly. "I wanted to invite him here before but I was afraid you would react like this, without even knowing him."

But the mention of Calvin's name was enough to clear the air. "Oh, if he's a friend of Calvin's, that's different. Why didn't you say so in the first place?"

Pauline gave Robin a long, suffering look and sighed without answering. In any case, she didn't need to reply because the phone rang and Mrs. Dahlgren was called out of the room.

Robin was just starting to inquire about Michael, whom she had always liked, when they were interrupted by a loud cry of anguish. Rushing into the hall, they saw Mrs. Dahlgren by the phone with her hand clapped to her head and her face contorted as if in pain.

"Mother, what on earth is it?" Pauline's eyes widened. "Not Dad . . ."

"Or Dicky . . ." Robin whispered.

"It's awful! They can't come—either of them," Mrs. Dahlgren wailed.

The two girls looked at each other blankly. "Who can't come?"

"Violet and Catherine." When that still didn't produce any reaction, Mrs. Dahlgren added impatiently, "The girls who were going to give out the leis."

"Do you mean to tell me you scared us out of our wits over a little thing like *that?*" Pauline demanded.

Her mother was indignant. "It isn't a little thing—it's the tiny details that are important. I've told you that over and over. Oh, this just spoils everything," she wailed.

"You're getting upset over absolutely nothing," Pauline remarked. "All you have to do is call the caterers and have them send two more girls."

"They didn't come from the caterer and that's not the problem anyway. We have plenty of help. These girls were to circulate among the guests wearing those colorful little sarong-type things with flowers in their hair."

Her daughter looked incredulous and slowly shook her head. "You're amazing, do you know that? You've just set women's lib back one hundred years."

"Pauline, I have no time to listen to your foolishness right now," Mrs. Dahlgren snapped. She pursed her lips and her brow furrowed in thought. "I have the costumes—now where can I get two girls at this hour?"

"Perhaps if you called them back they could suggest someone," Robin offered.

The older woman shook her head. "No, they would have—" Suddenly she broke off, and her gaze focused on Robin as though noticing her for the first time. She studied the girl for a long moment, then a smile cleared her face like the sun chasing away a cloud. "My dear, how would you like to do me the most stupendous favor?"

"Mother, you aren't suggesting . . . ?" Pauline was aghast.

"Well, why not? Robin would look adorable in that little outfit—the blue one to match her eyes, I think. I'm sure she wouldn't mind, would you, dear?"

"How can you even consider such a thing. She isn't a *servant!*"

"Oh, Pauline, don't be so tedious. I don't want her to do any actual work—the caterer's people will do that. All I'm asking is that she mingle with the guests and be her own sweet, charming self." Looking critically at Robin, she said, "I must say I've never seen a blond Hawaiian, but I daresay no one will notice."

Pauline faced her mother with blazing eyes. "I won't let you do this to her—it's degrading and . . . and downright stupid!"

Mrs. Dahlgren's frayed temper snapped at the same moment. "How dare you talk to me that way? One more word out of you and I'll speak to your father. I won't have you spoiling this party."

"You're the one who is ruining everything!" Pauline cried.

Robin was acutely embarrassed, especially since she was the cause of this angry scene. The thought of wearing that skimpy outfit in front of a bunch of strangers was extremely distasteful, but she knew that Mrs. Dahlgren would now consider it a point of pride not to back down. She also knew how much this evening meant to Pauline and she couldn't bear to see it spoiled for her. What difference does it really make, she thought. I don't know any of them so it doesn't matter how I look. The only trouble was that she had hoped to slip away early in the evening. Now she would have to stay till the bitter end. Oh, well, she could get through it somehow. Pauline's immediate defense of her had touched Robin deeply and it was a small sacrifice to make in return.

"Look, it doesn't matter," she told them. "We're all tired and we're getting excited over nothing. I'll be happy to fill in. It will be sort of fun," she told Pauline, managing not to choke on the lie.

Her friend looked at her suspiciously. "I know you better than that."

"No, really, I mean it," Robin assured her.

"You don't have to do it if you don't want to." Pauline remained unconvinced.

Robin avoided a direct answer by linking her arm in Pauline's. "Come on—let's all go take a little rest before it's time to get ready for the party. We've earned it."

When Robin got out of the shower a little later, she found her costume laid out on the bed. Regarding it with distaste, she still had to admit that it was a beautiful print. Called a pareu by the Hawaiians, it was a short sarong-type garment that wrapped to one side, leaving the shoulders bare and a long expanse of leg equally so. This one had a white background with brilliant large blue flowers splashed across it, the centers a mixture of black and yellow.

It took a few false starts to get the hang of it, but she finally managed to drape it correctly around her slender figure. Giving the ends an extra tug for security, she looked at herself in the mirror. Even she had to admit the effect wasn't half bad. The bright color accentuated the golden tan of her bare shoulders and the short skirt showed off her slim legs to advantage. Turning critically, she surveyed the deep slit that showed off a full half of her left thigh. It was much higher than she would have liked, but no amount of tugging would close the skirt, so she had to resign herself. There were no shoes to go with the outfit. Instead, there was one anklet of fresh blossoms on an elastic band, and Robin realized she was supposed to go barefoot. Well, at least I'll be comfortable, she rationalized.

Music had been wafting up the staircase for some time and she knew the moment couldn't be put off any longer. Checking her image one last time in the mirror, she noticed a vase of flowers on her dresser. Remembering Mrs. Dahlgren's instructions, she plucked a large white hibiscus flower with a yellow stamen and tucked it behind her left ear. The color blended into her pale hair, but it would have to do because it was the only kind she had in the room and there was no time to go out to the garden to pick another. The fragile white bloom was better suited to the raven tresses of Violet or Catherine. Lucky for me there wasn't time or Mrs. Dahlgren might have made me dye my hair black, Robin thought. Laughing to herself, she ran lightly down the stairs.

Mrs. Dahlgren was bustling about needlessly, since everything was under control. The house looked beautiful, with twinkling candles sending a shimmering glow that was unmistakably festive. Unobtrusive maids in black uniforms with white organdy aprons were checking the hors d'oeuvres and two bartenders had set up shop both inside and out on the patio. A Hawaiian steel band was responsible for the pulsating music filling the air.

"Oh, Robin, thank goodness you're ready. Let me look at you." Mrs. Dahlgren inspected her closely and was satisfied with the result. "You look absolutely marvelous! You see, I was right, wasn't I?" Without waiting for an answer she said, "Here are the boxes of leis—you know what to do"—and she was gone.

It was only a matter of minutes before the doorbell rang and the first guests started to arrive. One of the black-garbed maids answered the door, but it was Robin's job to greet them.

"Aloha," she said, smiling, slipping a flower lei over each head and kissing each guest on the cheek as she had been instructed.

At first it was sort of fun, but as they started to arrive in droves, her smile became rather fixed. Even so, it wasn't too bad until a large man in a Stetson hat came in. She gave the standard greeting and pecked him on the cheek but he grabbed her and held her close.

"Just a minute, little missy, you call that a proper kiss?"

"It's an old Hawaiian custom," she said, struggling to free herself.

"Let me show you how we do it back where I come from," he said, holding on to her.

Robin's cheeks were flushed as she tried to push him away without making a scene. He was like an overgrown bear, and she wasn't getting anyplace until suddenly a hand clamped down on his shoulder and an authoritative voice said, "I think the lady wants you to let go."

Calvin was looking at the man with steely eyes, and although his tone was suave, there was no mistaking his intentions.

After a brief pause, the man released her. "Shoot. I was just having a little fun," he said, backing away.

Robin looked up at Calvin with gratitude. Part of her mind couldn't help registering how handsome he looked, his deep tan accentuated by the snowy shirt-front. "Thank you—that was getting a little awkward."

"Glad to be of assistance," he said. She waited for him to move away but he just stood there. When she looked uncertainly at him, he smiled and said, "I'll take a white one—it matches my shirt."

"Wha . . . what?" And then she realized he was talking about the flowers. Selecting a lei, she placed it around his neck.

"How about the old Hawaiian custom?"

Blushing furiously, she stood on tiptoe and kissed him on both cheeks. His skin was smooth beneath her trembling lips and she was acutely conscious of the warmth generating from him.

"Thank you," he said, and some unreadable emotion flickered in his eyes.

She turned away in confusion and was relieved to find the next guest was Michael Browning. "It's so good to see you," she exclaimed. "Pauline told me the big news—about your leaving the ship," she added, as he looked startled. "You'll have to tell me all about what you're doing now."

He took her hand and squeezed it. "Yes, we'll have to have a long talk. Pauline told me what good friends you two are and I hope we will be too."

He was gone before Robin could sort out that rather puzzling remark—she had thought they were already friends. Oh, well, people say all kinds of trivial things at parties, she thought. The crush of guests soon erased it from her mind.

Eventually everyone arrived and was duly greeted. Robin's job was over and she started to wonder what the chances would be of following her earlier plan and quietly slipping away, but it wasn't to be.

Mrs. Dahlgren came looking for her. "Come along, dear, there are some people who want to meet you. You did a fine job and I'm really pleased. Everyone says the leis were a delightful touch."

Robin, following dutifully in her wake, did her best to be charming to a lot of people she didn't know. Surreptitiously she glanced around for Pauline and Calvin, but neither were to be found. It was an ache she determinedly pushed to the back of her mind.

The evening seemed to go on and on until Robin thought it would never end. After a while she saw Pauline dancing with Calvin. She was looking over his shoulder and when she spotted Robin made a circle with her thumb and forefinger indicating approval. But it wasn't until later, after Pauline had danced with Michael, that the two girls had a chance for a word together.

The combo had ended a set and were taking a short intermission. Pauline called to her as she strolled off the floor hand in hand with Michael, and Robin excused herself from a group and went to meet them.

"You look really darling," Pauline told her generously, "and comfortable too. I wish I were barefoot." She eyed her spike-heeled silver sandals ruefully.

Robin looked at her friend, who was shimmering like a Christmas angel, with a face just as radiant. "It's worth a little discomfort to look as beautiful as you do tonight." She appealed to Michael. "Isn't it?"

His glance was eloquent. Reaching out a tentative hand, he touched Pauline's hair gently, as though it were made of spun sugar. They smiled at each other and Robin got a lump in her throat. Poor Michael—he must be in love with Pauline. Didn't he know she was Calvin's? Unfortunately, falling in love wasn't some-

thing you had any control over—she could certainly
testify to that.

Unaware of all the feelings she was churning up,
Pauline inspected Robin with interest. "I suppose with
her passion for authenticity, it was Mother's idea for
you to go barefoot, wasn't it?" she asked, and laughed
when Robin nodded. "Well, don't tell her, but I think
you have your flower behind the wrong ear." When
they both looked inquiringly at her, she explained,
"Everything in Hawaiian lore has a meaning—you
know, like all those hand movements in the hula. A
flower worn behind the left ear means a girl is spoken
for but if it's behind the right ear it means she's still
looking—so you'd better be careful. One of these men
might take you seriously."

"There is no one here tonight I really fancy, so I'd
better change it," Robin laughed, "but not right this
minute. It's pinned in and I'd have to comb my hair all
over again."

"All right, but don't say I didn't warn you," Pauline
told her as the music started and she and Michael
drifted off to dance again.

Mrs. Dahlgren was beckoning to her across the room
and Robin sighed and prepared to go back into the
fray. There was only one good thing about it—as
Pauline pointed out, her feet didn't hurt.

"It's time to start the entertainment," Mrs. Dahlgren
told her. "Will you try and get everyone together?"

In keeping with the native theme of the party, a
Hawaiian show was to be presented. Folding chairs had
been unobtrusively set up around the patio and Robin
guided the guests to their seats. It was a picture book
setting with moonlight supplemented by flaming torches lighting the terrace.

When the last guest had found a place to sit, the band struck up a standard Hawaiian tune. Two women in hula skirts and garlands of flowers began to tell a story with their hands and arms while their hips swayed to the lilting music. Robin had seen the hula many times by now, but it never failed to delight her—especially the dancers' graceful movements. Her favorite was the tale of a fish swimming in the sea, portrayed by undulating movements of a slender arm and cupped fingers.

After several numbers, the women were replaced by two men, who performed the Polynesian fire dance. This music was much more stirring and even the guests moved in time to its primitive beat. Robin had found an unobtrusive corner near the wall and was giving the dancers her rapt attention, her lips slightly parted and unaware that Calvin's eyes returned often to her delicate face.

On stage, the men leaped and whirled, their fiery torches making glowing pinwheels as they swung them in the air. It was an exciting dance and their efforts brought a prolonged round of applause from an appreciative audience.

The last act was a man and a woman singing all the native favorites. Their voices blended in sweet harmony as they sang of pearly bubbles and little grass shacks. Swaying gently to the beat, they made a pretty picture with their flashing teeth and exotic good looks.

As a finale, they drifted into the "Hawaiian Wedding Song," and the pure notes commanded complete silence. "I do love you" the girl sang and Robin felt tears prickle her eyelids. It's only an act, she told herself, but the two young people were looking at each other as if they really meant it. Those beautiful words promising love and trust forever floated on the still night air. Unfortunately, Robin no longer believed in fairy tales.

When the show was over, everyone started to talk at once, complimenting Mrs. Dahlgren, commenting on the performers, and just chatting in general. They were apparently unaffected by the last song, but it had left Robin inexpressibly sad. Feeling the urgent need for a quiet moment alone, she waited until Mrs. Dahlgren's back was turned and inched her way through the crowd.

"No thank you, not right now," she told the man who wanted to dance with her, and, "I'll be right back," she assured another.

There were people everywhere, but Robin knew of a dark corner screened off by some tall bushes. Too late, she realized it was already occupied. Someone else had the same need for a breather. She stopped in her tracks as she recognized the someone as Calvin—perhaps the last person in the world she wanted to see after the tender love song. He didn't seem overjoyed to see her either, but he patted the low stone wall next to him and said pleasantly enough, "Come and join me."

She half turned away but he reached out and clamped his hand around her wrist. "Just once I wish I didn't have to hold on to you. When are you going to stop being such a child? You were looking for a quiet place and this is the only one there is."

Robin didn't know how to retreat without provoking a further outburst, so she gingerly perched on the stone wall next to him. Only then did she realize how tired she was.

"You made quite a hit in there," he remarked.

"I wouldn't say that. It was just a crazy idea of Mrs. Dahlgren's. I did it to please her."

"I know. Pauline told me."

"Where is Pauline?" she asked, wondering for the first time what he was doing out here alone.

"She's dancing with Michael," he said carelessly.

Of course he's unconcerned, Robin thought. He knows he has nothing to worry about. She wished the party was over—her legs ached and so did her spirits. Raising one knee, she absentmindedly started to rub her ankle.

He looked at her searchingly. "Tired?" When she nodded her head, he reached down and scooped her legs up onto his lap, then started to massage her bare feet with strong fingers.

Startled, she tried to free her legs, but he held on to them. "Surely it doesn't bother you when I touch your *feet?*" he asked.

"It doesn't bother me when you touch me anywhere," she said hotly, and then was furious at herself for putting it that way—especially after his low chuckle.

"Then relax and enjoy it." His hands were strong and sure as he moved them in long, firm strokes from her ankles to her aching calves.

"Suppose someone came along and saw us?"

"They might think I was trying to seduce you," he conceded. "But they would probably be sorry they hadn't thought of it first."

She wrenched her legs away and stood up. "You must be insane! Suppose Pauline saw us?"

"I don't think Pauline would jump to any conclusions—nor would she sit in judgment. Unlike you, she isn't a prude."

Robin couldn't believe her ears! He was within hours of becoming engaged to a wonderful girl, yet it didn't bother him a bit to betray her. He even thought she'd forgive him—that's how sure of himself he was. One last fling, was that it? But how could he think Robin would be a party to it?

Poor Pauline. Someone ought to tell her what she was getting into, but Robin knew she could never do it. It would hurt her too much and she might not even believe it. He certainly had all bases covered. They say love is blind, and one look at Pauline's radiant face testified that she trusted her lover implicitly. Robin could never say anything bad about Calvin to her dear friend, but at least she could tell him he didn't have *everybody* fooled.

"You're a monster, do you know that?" she cried. "You don't deserve anyone kind and decent. You talk so easily of love but I don't think you even know what it is. Have you ever really experienced true love? I'm sure you haven't," she said scornfully. "There is only one thing on your mind."

He sprang to his feet and his face frightened her. She had never seen anyone so furiously angry. He grabbed her bare shoulders and held her in an iron grip, his fingers making deep indentations in her soft flesh.

"You have the nerve to ask me if I've ever been in love? What would you know about it? Have you ever had an honest emotion in your life that you didn't try to suppress or ignore?"

He was like a tiger glaring at his prey and Robin was terribly afraid, but she summoned all her courage to say, "I know there is more to love than sex, no matter what you say."

His fingers bit even deeper. "Are you truly as naive

as you sound? I don't think so. I think you're scared of life." He gave her a little shake. "Why are you afraid to grow up? There is a whole world out there and I could have shown it to you, but I can't reach you." His eyes were bleak as he added softly, "God knows I've tried!"

"Yes, you've tried," she cried passionately. "I practically told you how inexperienced I was and you used that knowledge to play on my emotions, to make me do things I can't even bear to think about."

For one terrible moment she thought he was going to strike her. "What does it take to awaken you? Evidently a better man than I am."

"You're right! And someday I'll meet that man," she told him bravely, knowing all the while that it was a lie. There would never be anyone like him. For the rest of her life she would measure every man against his giant image—and they would all be found wanting.

At that, his fingers loosed their terrible grip. All the fire was gone from his eyes and he looked immeasurably weary. "So this is the way it ends," he said quietly. "I'm going away tomorrow." He looked at her searchingly. "You do know this is goodbye, don't you?"

She nodded her head through a blur of tears. They stood there looking at each other wordlessly and then he gathered her in his arms and kissed her so hard that she could feel his teeth pressed against her lips, bruising her mouth. Her arms were imprisoned against his chest and he lifted her off her feet, holding her as if he would never let go. Just as suddenly he released her, and Robin had to put her hand out to steady herself or she would have fallen, but he made no move to catch her.

The tears were welling up now but she had to convince him they were tears of anger not of grief.

Thinking wildly of a way to wound him, she cried, "You're still the macho male, aren't you? Taking whatever you want because you know I can't stop you."

One eyebrow rose sardonically and he said, "Not this time, my love. This time you asked for it yourself." And reaching out, he pulled the blossom from her hair. "It's an old Hawaiian custom." His mouth twisted bitterly and he turned abruptly and disappeared into the night.

Chapter Nine

The rhythmic beat of a Hawaiian song filled the air, but Robin heard it as if from a great distance. Her shoulders still bore the imprint of his fingers and her bruised mouth ached from his kiss. She sank slowly down onto the low stone wall, her knees no longer able to support her. He was gone forever and she felt a desolation as deep as the grave.

Why? her tired mind demanded. He confused and tormented her. He ignored her one moment and reduced her to abject slavery the next, with one touch of his hand, one look from those dark eyes that could be so kind and then so cruel. Why can't I realize how lucky I am that he's gone? But the finality of never seeing him again caused a crushing pain in her breast.

A cloud passed over the moon and now the sky was lit only by icy, splintered stars. The dancers started to go inside and the musicians began to pack up their

174

instruments, but Robin didn't notice. She continued to sit there, filled with misery and doubt.

Could she bear to let him walk out of her life thinking she was cold and unfeeling? Oh, if he only knew how she *really* felt. How much was pride worth? But what difference did it make? He belonged to Pauline, her dearest friend, whom she would never do anything to hurt. No, it was better this way. Let him think what he liked. If he knew how she actually felt it would make him uncomfortable at best. After all, he had turned her down once, hadn't he? She at least had that to be grateful for, although she would never understand it.

"Robin, Robin, where are you?" Gradually she realized that someone was calling her name, and had been for some minutes. It was Mrs. Dahlgren and her voice was the only one to be heard. The party was evidently over.

Robin got stiffly to her feet and went into the house.

"There you are! Where on earth have you been? I've been looking for you for hours. I can't find Pauline either. I declare, you two girls are like a couple of eels in the ocean. If I take my eyes off you for one second, you slide out of sight." Robin murmured something noncommittal, but Mrs. Dahlgren wasn't really waiting for an answer, she was merely letting off steam after the excitement of the evening. "I think everyone had a good time, but now that it's over, I believe I'm going to simply collapse." She looked ruefully around at the debris that is the aftermath of every party, no matter how elegant.

"Why don't you go on to bed," Robin told her. "I'll straighten up down here."

"That's awfully good of you, my dear, but you must be tired too."

"No, not very," Robin lied.

"You young people are wonderful," Mrs. Dahlgren said gratefully. "I just wish I had half your energy."

After she left, Robin gathered up used glasses and cocktail napkins. There were also dirty ashtrays to be emptied and a few cushions to be fluffed up. Although she was bone weary, Robin knew that sleep was out of the question, so she was glad to have something to do. It was while she was carrying a tray of glasses to the kitchen that a piercing scream rang out upstairs. After almost dropping the tray, she set it down hurriedly and rushed up the staircase.

Through the open door of the Dahlgren suite, she could see Mr. Dahlgren trying to comfort his wife, who was having hysterics.

Robin ran into the room and confronted them. "What's wrong? What happened?" But they could barely hear her through the noise of Mrs. Dahlgren's shrieks.

"You musn't do this, my dear," Mr. Dahlgren said. "You'll make yourself ill." The only effect of his words was to make her sob harder.

"What's wrong?" Robin repeated, but again they didn't answer her.

Mrs. Dahlgren was clutching a piece of paper and she waved it in the air. "How could she do this to me? Oh, that treacherous girl. What have I done to deserve this?"

It was hard to make out her words through the torrent of tears but gradually Robin got the impression that, whatever it was, it involved Pauline.

"Has something happened to her?" she asked fearfully.

Mr. Dahlgren finally became aware of her presence

and turned to her with relief. "I'm afraid Margaret is a little upset." That was the understatement of the year! "Maybe you can calm her down."

Robin put her arm around the distraught woman. "Tell me what it is—maybe I can help." As this only led to further wails, Robin led her to a chaise and made her lie down. "Did something happen to Pauline? Please tell me," she begged Mr. Dahlgren.

He looked extremely uncomfortable—almost shame-faced—and Robin was wild with worry. But before he could answer her question, his wife started her lament all over again. "My only daughter, how could she do it? I've always dreamed of seeing Pauline as a bride and now it will never happen."

Robin turned cold at those awful words. She was so distracted she actually shook her employer. "What is it—you have to tell me!"

Mrs. Dahlgren's sobs gave way to high-pitched mirthless laughter as her eyes finally focused on Robin. "It's very simple. Pauline has eloped—that's what happened." Then the tears started again. "I won't ever see her walk down the aisle with bridesmaids and a flower girl. I've been planning her wedding since the day she was born and now . . . here, here, read it yourself." She waved the piece of paper at Robin, who recoiled as if it were a snake.

Pauline married! I thought it was going to be an engagement party, but it was actually her wedding night, she thought. No wonder she insisted on a white dress—it was her wedding gown! Mrs. Dahlgren might have been cheated out of the big church ceremony she had her heart set on, but at least she got to see her daughter dressed in white, Robin thought wildly.

"I wish you wouldn't carry on like this, Margaret,"

Mr. Dahlgren said helplessly. "Doesn't it mean anything that she married a fine man and she's happy?"

This only brought on further paroxysms of grief, and
Robin took the moment to escape. The house was
closing around her and she thought she was going to
suffocate. Running barefoot down the stairs, she slid
open the wide patio windows and gulped in the fresh
night air. The beach was deserted but palm trees
rustled and whispered to each other while huge break-
ers crashed on the sand, their white crests dissipating
into swirling foam. All of nature seemed to be forming
a Greek chorus as a background to Mrs. Dahlgren's
grief.

Robin wandered down to the hard-packed sand.
Cool water soothed her feet and she stood there
watching the tide grasp futilely at the shore. As each
wave rolled onto the beach and then retreated, she
sank deeper and deeper into the clutching sand until
her feet were buried up to the ankles. If I stood here
long enough, would I be buried completely, she
wondered? The idea was tempting. Never to feel lost or
lonely again—just to close her eyes and stop caring
. . . She gave a shiver and yanked her feet out of the
clinging ooze, then turned and walked slowly down the
beach.

There were lights in Calvin's house and she drifted in
that direction, drawn irresistibly. Were they there now,
he and Pauline? It wasn't likely. Perhaps they were on
Kauai at his beautiful resort. When he said, "I'm
leaving tomorrow," she didn't realize he had meant on
his honeymoon.

The sand beneath her feet changed from wet to damp
and then to powdery dry as she moved slowly toward
the house, knowing it was insane but unable to stop

herself. The pool lights had been turned off and the whole outside area was in darkness, but the lovely oval gleamed faintly in the starlight. Robin had no clear idea of why she was here. She was like a sleepwalker unconsciously seeking the two people she loved best in the world.

When a voice spoke almost at her side, she was startled out of a trancelike state and her heart began to race wildly.

"What are you doing here?" It was Calvin's voice, calm and faintly disinterested.

Robin peered into the darkness and saw him lying on a chaise, arms folded on his chest. "You . . . you startled me."

"No doubt. I didn't exactly expect to see you either," he told her drily.

She looked wildly around for Pauline, horribly embarrassed at having interrupted them on their wedding night of all times! But Pauline was nowhere in sight. Undoubtedly she was in the bedroom changing into the beautiful satin nightgown that Robin had helped her select. Robin's cheeks flamed and she couldn't help glancing toward the house.

"What are you looking for?" Calvin asked.

"I . . . I thought Pauline might be here." She swallowed hard, wondering what kind of excuse she could trump up for wanting to see her friend at this hour.

But when he answered, there was surprise in his voice. "Pauline? What would she be doing here?"

Now Robin was truly confused, but she didn't feel that she could ask for an explanation. The best thing to do would be to leave them alone and hope they didn't think she was too big an idiot.

She started to back away in confusion but Calvin

stopped her. Unfolding his long legs, he got up from the chaise. "Wait a minute. Why did you think you would find Pauline here?"

"I thought . . . I thought maybe you might spend your first night here," she mumbled, too miserable to meet his eye.

He was incredulous. "Pauline and *me?*" he exclaimed. "Where on earth would you get an idea like that?"

"The note . . . I mean, Mrs. Dahlgren said . . ." Robin knew she was being incoherent, so she tried again. "Pauline left her mother a note saying she had eloped." There, it was out.

He looked at her for a long uncomprehending minute and then started to laugh. "Pauline eloped tonight, all right, but not with me."

For a minute she could only stare at him, not believing her ears. Then, remembering the scene in Mrs. Dahlgren's bedroom, Robin realized that Pauline's mother never actually said who she had eloped with. She had waved the note at her, but Robin, after jumping to an obvious conclusion, had been too heartsick to read it. Now she put both hands over her mouth in sudden horror. Pauline had jilted him and run off with someone else! Poor Calvin, how this must hurt. No wonder the engagement was never announced, it now occurred to her.

She held her hands out in a gesture of compassion. "I'm sorry," she said simply.

"About what?"

"About you and Pauline."

"There's nothing to be sorry about," he told her. "I don't know where you got the idea, but there has never been anything between us except affection. I feel like an uncle toward her and all her clan."

"But she's in love with *you*," Robin cried and then stopped in confusion. "At least she was."

"What gave you that notion?"

"She told me so. She said she adored you."

Calvin laughed. "You know Pauline—that's just the way she talks. I hate to explode your romantic little fantasy, my dear, but Pauline has been in love with Michael Browning since the day she met him on the ship coming over here."

"Michael!" Suddenly memories came flooding over Robin. Michael and Pauline sitting very close together on the float, walking hand in hand down the beach. And the most telling indication of all—the way they had looked at each other tonight when he reached out to touch her—as though she were something rare and precious. Why hadn't she guessed? It was her own fault. Pauline had tried to tell her but she wouldn't listen. Robin was remembering that day in the shopping center when Pauline was bursting with confidences that she was unwilling to hear.

"Now I understand why Mrs. Dahlgren was so upset tonight," Robin said slowly. "I thought it was because she felt cheated out of a big wedding but that wasn't it at all."

Calvin grinned. "No. I'm afraid it was the choice of bridegrooms that undid her. I rather think I was slated for the top slot." Robin nodded and he continued, "Pauline knew her mother wouldn't approve of Michael, so she never brought him around. They met at my house and at first I didn't think anything of it. I knew they were in love but I didn't realize they were that serious. As soon as I found out they intended to get married, I made Pauline tell her father. I would never have been a party to deceiving her parents and I assumed he would pave the way with her mother. Obviously he didn't, but he must have had his reasons."

Robin knew that Mrs. Dahlgren would have moved heaven and earth to break up the romance and her husband must have known it also. But Michael was a fine man and he was Pauline's choice.

"I suppose he just wanted her to be happy," Robin said, and then a thought occurred that brought a small frown to her delicate brows. "But what are they going to live on? He gave up his job on the ship to be with her and now what will happen? I don't think Pauline has any money of her own, and she's never worked a day in her life. Oh, dear!" Her happiness was marred by concern for her best friend.

"Don't worry about them—they'll be fine. He has a better job." At Robin's doubtful look he added reluctantly, "Michael is going to work for me."

"But he's a sailor—that's all he knows how to do," Robin fretted.

"As it happens, the captain of my yacht has been ailing and I've been thinking of getting someone to assume part of his duties and eventually take over. Mike is made to order for the job and it will be better for Pauline too. He won't be off to sea for weeks at a time."

"Oh, Calvin, you're really wonderful," Robin told him, relieved and happy for her dear friend.

"Now you sound like Pauline. Am I to infer that you're in love with me too?" His tone was casual but his gaze was intent on her.

She stared back at him. For the first time it occurred to her that he was free! He wasn't in love with Pauline—he wasn't in love with anyone.

That last thought caused her heart to plummet as fast as it had soared. For just a moment she had dared to hope, but nothing had really changed. Remembering his bitter words to her on the Dahlgren patio, she recognized how futile her dreams were. With drooping shoulders she stared misty-eyed at this dark pirate looming so tall. He would go through life enslaving girls like herself and then casting them aside, but even knowing that didn't make any difference in her feelings. Yes, I love you, she thought, and may heaven help me.

"I seem to have the knack of upsetting you," he said, making no move to touch her. "But will you tell me why you're crying now?"

The night turned her eyes to navy blue pools brimming with crystal tears. "What difference does it make? We've said our goodbyes. I couldn't bear to go through it again."

"Does that mean you care that I'm leaving?" He watched her like a giant cat playing with a very fragile little mouse.

Why did he always demand more than she wanted to give? Why couldn't he just once be gentle with her? She swayed forward, wanting him to take her in his arms yet hating herself for being so weak. Would it be so terrible, though, to ask for his touch just one more time?

As if divining her thoughts, he shook his head. "No, that would be too easy. This time you have to say it yourself." His face was cruel and expressionless, draining her of all pride. "Say it!" he commanded. "Tell me how you feel."

She started to tremble, caught in his inexorable web. "I . . . I . . ."

Her eyes were wide and frightened but he ignored their mute appeal. "Say it, Robin. As God is my judge, this is your last chance!"

She looked into his blazing eyes and the words were drawn out almost against her will. "I love you," she whispered.

There was wild exultation in his face as he ordered, "Say it again!"

"I love you." Her voice was stronger and the words seemed to echo joyously in the friendly night—*I love you, I love you, I love you!*

He made a sound like a sob deep in his throat and gathered her into his arms. "Darling, I never thought I'd hear that." His mouth sought hers and the kisses were tender and gentle as his lips roamed along the soft curve of her cheek, her eyelids, and back to her lips once more.

Robin clung to him in ecstasy, almost afraid to breathe for fear it would turn out to be a dream. If it is, please don't let me wake up, she begged silently.

He rested his cheek against her shining hair. "If you only knew how I've longed for this moment."

She gave a small moan of pure contentment. "Me too," she breathed.

"Then why . . ." He stopped to kiss her temple. "Why did you let me give up hope? Do you know I really intended to leave tomorrow because I couldn't bear to be near you any longer knowing I could never have you?" The thought was too terrible to contemplate and Robin closed her eyes and snuggled closer. "Why didn't you say something?" he asked.

She stirred in his arms and looked up at him shyly.

"How could I tell you? You were always so cruel, mocking me and talking about . . . about . . ." She lowered her head.

He put his finger under her chin, forcing her to look at him. "Didn't you know why?" When she shook her head, he went on, "You were such a baby—you thought sex was something people practiced on Mars. I know how young and inexperienced you are, but I wanted a wife, not a child bride who thought it would be fun to play house. A lot of women have wanted to be Mrs. Calvin Carrington III—I want a girl who wants *me*."

Robin drew away from him slightly. "You knew I didn't feel that way," she protested. "I fell in love with you when I thought you were just a sailor. That's the way this whole thing started."

He kissed the tip of her nose. "I know, my pet, but you were so frightened every time I touched you. I want to make love to you and have you return my love. I want to hold you in my arms and make you part of me."

She hid her burning face in his throat and her whispered words were barely audible. "I want that too."

"Oh, my darling!" He held her so close that she could feel his heart pounding.

A sudden thought occurred to her. "But that night on Kauai . . . that night I . . ." She couldn't go on.

He looked at her grimly. "You little devil, you don't know what you almost precipitated that night. I knew what you were doing, but I'm only human you know!"

"You were so angry," she breathed.

"Of course I was angry! That was a damn fool stunt and I should have tanned your little bottom." He looked at her tenderly. "I wanted a wife, not a mistress—didn't you know that, you precious baby?"

Suddenly the enormity of it swept over Robin. He was actually asking her to marry him! All the misery and doubt were gone and the future that had appeared so dark now looked like the ending to a fairy tale. But it wasn't the end, it was only the beginning. There is a whole world out there, he had told her, and now she would see it with him.

Robin sighed contentedly. "Do you think Pauline and Michael are as blissful right now as we are?"

"How could they be? We've cornered the happiness market." He stroked her hair. "Although hard as it is to believe, I'm sure they feel exactly the way we do." A glint of deviltry lit his eyes. "The only one who lost in this deal is Pauline's mother."

"Oh, poor Mrs. Dahlgren. I wonder whether she's still having hysterics." Robin laughed in spite of herself. "And I'll have to give notice, which isn't going to make her wildly happy either." The world started to intrude and she realized there were plans to be made. "Do you think a month would be fair?"

He frowned. "No, I don't think that would be fair at all."

Robin was taken aback. She had dreamed for so long about being his wife that even a month seemed achingly long, but evidently he felt that wasn't enough. "How much time do you think I should give?" she asked uncertainly.

"I had in mind about twelve hours."

"Twelve hours? What are you saying?" She was incredulous.

"If you think I'm going to wait a month for you—or even a day, for that matter—you're out of your lovely little mind. I'm not going to take the chance of letting you get away from me again. You're mine now and don't you ever forget it."

"But I can't just walk out on her," Robin protested.

He was completely unmoved by the prospect, "Mrs. Dahlgren is an able-bodied woman, perfectly capable of taking care of her own son. In fact, it will do her a world of good."

"But it seems so—"

"I have two tickets to Marbella on the morning flight," he interrupted her. "We'll be married as soon as we land." He looked at her with laughing eyes. "Do you know how to say 'I do' in Spanish?" And before she could reply, he told her, "It doesn't matter, you can just nod your head."

"Marbella," she breathed. "It sounds like a suburb of heaven."

"It's a wonderful place for a honeymoon," he assured her. "I have a villa there that's high on a hill. You can see for miles and the air is scented with jasmine. It's surrounded by a stone wall, and when we get there I'm going to close the gates and have you all to myself."

Robin's eyelashes fluttered shyly before the passion in his gaze, but she leaned against him in complete surrender, anticipating the bliss that lay ahead.

Something he had said, though, echoed in a corner of her mind and she raised her head and asked, "Two tickets? Did you say you had two tickets?"

He kissed the tips of her fingers. "You see how I kept on hoping right up until the end? I was going to tear one up, but I couldn't bring myself to do it."

They looked deep into each other's eyes and Robin said simply, "I'm glad."

His strong, warm hand closed over hers, and he said, "Come on, before I test my willpower too much. I'm going to take you back to your single bed—for the last time."

Although she blushed a bright rosy pink, Robin had never felt more cherished and protected. She clung to his hand and tagged along after him down the beach the way she was willing to follow him for the rest of her life.

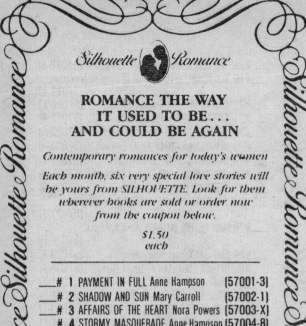

Silhouette 💮 _Romance_

ROMANCE THE WAY
IT USED TO BE...
AND COULD BE AGAIN

Contemporary romances for today's women

_Each month, six very special love stories will
be yours from SILHOUETTE. Look for them
wherever books are sold or order now
from the coupon below._

_$1.50
each_

SILHOUETTE BOOKS, Department SB/1

1230 Avenue of the Americas, New York, N.Y. 10020

Please send me the books I have checked above. I am enclosing $_____
(please add 50¢ to cover postage and handling for each order. N.Y.S. and N.Y.C.
residents please add appropriate sales tax). Send check or money order—no
cash or C.O.D.s please. Allow up to six weeks for delivery.

NAME_____

ADDRESS_____

CITY_____ STATE/ZIP_____

SB/10/80